FAIRY TALES
OF THE
BROTHERS GRIMM

FAIRY TALES
OF THE
BROTHERS
GRIMM

Retold and introduced by Neil Philip

Illustrated by Isabelle Brent

VIKING

VIKING

Published by the Penguin Group

Penguin Books USA Inc., 375 Hudson Street, New York, New York 10014, U.S.A.

Penguin Books Ltd., 27 Wrights Lane, London W8 5TZ, England

Penguin Books Australia Ltd., Ringwood, Victoria, Australia

Penguin Books Canada Ltd., 10 Alcorn Avenue, Toronto, Ontario, Canada M4V 3B2

Penguin Books (N.Z.) Ltd., 182-190 Wairau Road, Auckland 10, New Zealand

Penguin Books Ltd., Registered Offices: Harmondsworth, Middlesex, England

This edition first published in Great Britain by Little, Brown and Company (UK), 1997

First published in the United States of America by Viking,

a division of Penguin Books USA Inc., 1997

1 3 5 7 9 10 8 6 4 2

An Albion Book

ISBN: 0-670-87290-3

Library of Congress Catalog Card Number:

97-60082

Printed and bound in Hong Kong by South China Printing Co.

Typesetting by York House Typographic, London

For Aisling
N.P.

For Elisabeth Brent
I.B.

CONTENTS

INTRODUCTION

The collection of German fairy tales made at the beginning of the nineteenth century by the brothers Jacob and Wilhelm Grimm was the first work of its kind, and it remains the most famous. It has only one rival—the fairy tales of the Danish writer Hans Christian Andersen. But there is an essential difference between the two. Andersen made up his stories; the Grimms collected theirs from folk tradition.

This divide between Andersen's creative approach and the Grimms' scholarly one led to embarassment when Andersen called on the brothers unannounced in the summer of 1844. Though Andersen was already famous, Jacob had no idea who he was, and had never even heard his name. The Grimms later made friends with Andersen, and realized that they had even printed one of his stories, "The Princess and the Pea," in their 1843 edition, thinking it a genuine folktale.

The Grimms had published the first edition of their *Kinder- und*

Hausmärchen (Children's and Household Tales) in 1812, and continued revising and enlarging it until the seventh edition of 1857, which is the basis of most modern translations, and of my own free but faithful retellings. Their original aim was to record the folktales of Germany with unvarnished accuracy. This was a new and revolutionary idea, and it remains the foundation stone of all folktale research.

Some recent writers (such as John M. Ellis in his combative work *One Fairy Story Too Many: The Brothers Grimm and Their Tales*, 1983) have taken them to task for not carrying out this work with the strictness modern scholarship requires. They did not often identify their sources; they destroyed their manuscripts; they blended two or more tellings into single tales; and worst of all they continually tinkered with the language and even the plots of the tales to achieve maximum impact.

These criticisms are valid, but, as the essays in James M. McGlathery's excellent *The Brothers Grimm and Folktale* (1988) show, they have been taken too far. The Grimms had no model for their work; they had to invent the science of folklore as they went along. The final result may not be a word-for-word transcription of oral storytelling in a community, but it is nevertheless an authentic collection of genuine folk stories. Wilhelm Grimm—who was responsible for most of the writing and revision—was searching for a way to voice and shape traditional oral tales on the printed page. His lively versions triumphantly convey the directness and immediacy of oral storytelling, fixing the stories in a form that catches their essence and still speaks to us today.

Whatever its status as scholarship, the Grimms' collection of fairy tales is certainly a classic of children's literature. This new selection of stories contains some of their best-known tales, such as "The Frog Prince," "Rumpelstiltskin," and "Snow White," as well as some of their short comic stories, chosen to counter the widespread impression that all their tales are Grimm by name and grim by nature. There is cruelty and darkness in Grimm, but there is comedy and light as well.

The Grimms themselves were lifelong collaborators. Jacob, the more scholarly of the two, was born in 1785 and died in 1863. Wilhelm, the more literary, was born in 1786 and died in 1859. Their pioneering collections of German fairy tales and legends are not their only monument: they also initiated the great German dictionary, *Deutsches Wörterbuch*. When Wilhelm died, they had only reached the letter "D," and the massive project was not finally completed until 1961.

Jacob never married, but in 1825 Wilhelm married Dortchen Wild, from whom, when she was a girl, the brothers had recorded several stories, including "Rumpelstiltskin," "Many-furs," and "Mother Snow." Dortchen was, like many of the Grimms' sources, a middle-class girl; she was probably remembering the tales from the telling of her nurse.

The most famous of all the storytellers who contributed to the Grimms' collection was Dorothea Viehmann, from the village of Niederzwehren, near Cassel. The Grimms collected more than twenty tales from her, including "Clever Elsie," "The Peasant's Wise Daughter," "Hans the Hedgehog," "The Three Lazybones," and "The Miller's Boy and the Cat." Wilhelm called her the "fairytale-wife," and wrote, "She tells her stories with care, confidence, and great vitality, and enjoys doing so." Frau Viehmann was perhaps the most authentic folk storyteller among the Grimms' known sources; although John M. Ellis implies that her repertoire derived from the French stories of Charles Perrault, this is not true.

Another valued storyteller was the retired sergeant of dragoons Friedrich Krause, who told the Grimms the cheerfully amoral tale of "The Knapsack, the Hat, and the Horn" in exchange for an old pair of trousers.

One other story has a particularly interesting origin. The comic tale of "The Fisherman and His Wife," which is echoed in the first part of "The Gold Children," was collected by the Romantic painter Philipp Otto Runge, who recorded it in Pomeranian dialect. The wonderful descriptive detail in this well-rounded story may owe something to Runge's painter's eye. Recently Brian Alderson has translated this tale into Yorkshire dialect, and Gilbert McKay into Scots. Both these versions are well worth searching out—Alderson's in *The Brothers Grimm: Popular Folk Tales* (1978) and McKay's in *Jacob and Wilhelm Grimm: Selected Tales*, edited by David Luke (1982).

Whatever their sources, the Grimms' stories live in our minds because they take us deep into the fairy-tale world in which wishes come true, and the humble and the generous triumph over the mean and the proud. This is a world whose rules and customs the brothers Grimm well understood, and in which, thanks to their work, we can live happily for all our days.

THE FROG PRINCE

In the old days, when wishing still helped, there lived a king whose daughters were all beautiful, but the youngest was so beautiful that even the sun, who has seen so much, was amazed when he shone on her face.

Not far from the palace there was a great, dark forest, and under an old lime tree in the forest there was a spring. On hot days, the youngest princess used to go into the forest and sit beside the cool water, and when she was bored she took a golden ball and threw it into the air and caught it. It was her best-loved toy.

Now one day it so happened that the princess missed the ball, and it rolled into the spring. All the princess could do was watch it as it sank under the water and disappeared, for the spring was deep, so deep you couldn't see the bottom.

The princess began to cry. Her sobs grew louder and louder; she was in such distress. As she cried, she heard a voice saying,

"What's the matter, king's daughter? You are crying so hard, even a stone would pity you."

She looked where the voice was coming from, and saw a frog sticking its big ugly head out of the water.

"Oh! It's you, is it, splish-splash?" she said. "I am crying because my golden ball has fallen into the spring."

"Hush then, don't cry," said the frog. "I can help you. But what will you give me if I bring you back your toy?"

"Anything you like, you dear frog," she replied. "My clothes, my pearls, my jewels, even my golden crown."

"What do I care for your clothes, your pearls, your jewels, or your golden crown?" said the frog. "But if you will let me be your friend, and sit with you at table, and eat from your golden plate, and drink from your golden cup, and sleep in your bed, then I will dive down and fetch your golden ball."

"Oh yes," she said. "I promise!" But secretly she thought, *What nonsense this silly frog talks. All he does is sit in the water and croak. How could he be my friend?*

Once she had promised, the frog disappeared under the water and soon came back with the golden ball in its mouth and threw it on the grass.

The princess was so happy to have her toy back. She picked it up and ran off with it. The frog cried, "Wait! Take me with you. I can't run like you!" But no amount of croaking could make the princess listen. She was hurrying home and had already forgotten about the poor frog.

Next day, when the princess sat down at table with the king and all the courtiers, and was eating from her golden plate,

something came hopping, splish-splash, splish-splash, up the marble steps. When it came to the top, it knocked at the door, crying, "Princess, youngest princess, let me in."

She ran to see who was outside, and when she opened the door, she saw the frog. She slammed the door shut as fast as she could and sat down again. Her heart was beating so fast. The king could see she was scared. He said, "What are you afraid of, child? Is there a giant outside who wants to carry you off?"

"It's not a giant," she said. "It's a nasty, slimy frog."

"What does the frog want with you?"

"Oh, Father dear, yesterday when I was in the forest sitting by the spring, my golden ball fell into the water. Because I cried so, the frog fetched it out for me, but first it made me promise it could live with me and be my friend. I never thought it could get out of the spring, but now it's outside and wants to come in."

As they were speaking, the frog knocked a second time, calling,

> *Princess, youngest princess,*
> *Let me in.*
> *You gave me your promise,*
> *Down by the spring.*
> *Princess, youngest princess,*
> *Let me in.*

Then the king said, "You must keep your promises. Go and let it in." She went and opened the door and the frog hopped in and followed her, splish-splash, back to her chair.

Then the frog called, "Lift me up beside you." She didn't know what to do, but the king told her to lift it up.

Once he was on the chair, the frog said, "Push your golden plate nearer, so that we can eat together." With a bad grace, she did as he asked. The frog enjoyed his food, but every mouthful stuck in her throat.

At last the frog said, "I have eaten enough. Now I am tired, so carry me to your room and prepare your silken bed. Then we'll lie down and sleep."

The princess began to cry, because she was afraid of the cold frog. She didn't want to touch it, yet it wanted to sleep in her pretty, clean bed.

The king said angrily, "He helped you when you were in trouble, so you mustn't despise him now."

So she picked up the frog between the tips of two fingers, carried him upstairs, and dropped him in the corner. She got into bed and pulled the covers up tight, but the frog hopped, splish-splash, across the room, calling, "I'm tired, and I want to sleep in your bed. Lift me up or I shall tell your father."

She was so angry, she lifted the frog in both hands and hurled it against the wall. "That should shut you up, you horrible frog," she said.

But when the frog fell to the floor, he wasn't a frog anymore. He was a handsome prince with sparkling eyes. And it was her father's will that he should be her husband.

"A wicked witch put a spell on me," he said, "and only you could have broken it. Sleep now, and tomorrow I shall take you to my kingdom."

In the morning, a carriage arrived, drawn by eight white

horses with golden harnesses, and ostrich plumes in their head-bands. Behind them stood faithful Henry, the young prince's servant.

Faithful Henry had been so sad when his master was turned into a frog that he had had three iron bands forged around his heart, to stop it from bursting with grief. Now he had come in the carriage to take his master home. He helped the prince and princess into the carriage and stepped up behind them, full of joy.

After they had driven part of the way, the prince heard a great *crack*! He turned around, saying, "Henry, the carriage is breaking."

"No, master, it is an iron band that I had forged around my heart to keep it from breaking when you were turned into a frog and imprisoned in the spring."

Twice more on their journey the prince heard a *crack*! Twice more he thought the carriage was breaking. But it was only faithful Henry's heart filling with happiness, and snapping the iron bands of sorrow.

RAPUNZEL

There was once a man and a woman who longed in vain for a child. But at last it seemed as if God would answer their prayer.

From the window at the back of their house they could see a wonderful garden full of beautiful flowers and herbs. It was surrounded by a high wall, and no one dared go into it because it belonged to a powerful witch, and everyone was afraid of her.

One day the wife was standing by this window and looking down into the garden, when she caught sight of a lovely bed of rapunzel, which is a kind of lettuce. It looked so fresh and green it made her mouth water. Her craving for the rapunzel grew every day. It was so frustrating to be able to see it but never to eat it that she began to waste away. When her husband saw her so pale and wan, he asked, "What's wrong, darling?"

"Oh," she answered, "if I can't eat some of that rapunzel I shall die."

Her husband loved her, and he thought, *Sooner than let my wife die, I shall get her some of that rapunzel, whatever the cost.*

As dusk fell, he climbed over the wall into the witch's garden, snatched a handful of rapunzel, and took it to his wife. She made it into a salad straightaway and ate it greedily. It tasted good to her—so very good. The next day her craving was three times as great. It wouldn't let her rest.

There was nothing for it. The husband had to go back to the witch's garden. At dusk, he climbed the wall again. But when he came down on the other side, he nearly jumped out of his skin. There stood the witch, right in front of him!

She glared at him. "How dare you sneak into my garden and steal my rapunzel! I'll make you wish you hadn't."

"Have mercy," he pleaded. "I had to do it. My wife saw the rapunzel from our window, and she felt such a craving for it that she would have died if she hadn't got some to eat."

The witch's face softened. "If that's the case, I will let you pick as much rapunzel as you like, on one condition. When your wife's baby is born, you must give it to me. I will look after it and love it like a mother."

The man was so frightened he would have agreed to anything.

So when the baby was born, the witch came and took it away. It was a baby girl, and the witch called her Rapunzel.

Rapunzel grew into the most beautiful child under the sun. When she was twelve years old, the witch took her into the forest and shut her up in a tower that had neither stairs nor door, but only a little window right at the top. When the witch wanted to come in, she stood beneath it and called,

> *Rapunzel, Rapunzel,*
> *Let down your hair.*

Rapunzel had wonderful long hair, as fine as spun gold. When she heard the witch calling, she undid her braided tresses and let them tumble all the way to the ground so that the witch could climb up them.

A few years later, it happened that a prince was passing through the forest and rode by the tower. From it, he heard someone singing. It was Rapunzel, who often sang to herself. Her voice was so lovely and haunting that the prince stopped to listen. He wanted to climb up to her, but when he looked for the door to the tower, he could not find one. He rode away, but the singing had moved him so much that he came back every day to listen to it.

Once, when the prince was standing listening to Rapunzel's singing, the witch came. He heard her call,

> *Rapunzel, Rapunzel,*
> *Let down your hair.*

Then Rapunzel let down her tresses, and the witch climbed up to her.

Aha! he thought. *If that is the ladder by which I can climb up to her, then I will try my luck.* Next day, as dark fell, he went to the tower and called,

> *Rapunzel, Rapunzel,*
> *Let down your hair.*

The hair fell down, and he climbed up.

At first Rapunzel was terrified. She had never seen a man before. But the prince spoke so gently to her that she lost her fear. He said, "My heart was so moved by your singing that I could not rest. Please marry me."

He was so young and handsome, and Rapunzel thought he would love her more truly than the old witch. "Yes," she said. "I will marry you." And she gave him her hand.

Then Rapunzel said, "But how will I ever get down? . . . I know. Every time you come, you must bring a skein of silk, and then I can make a ladder with it. When it's finished, I will climb down, and you can carry me off on your horse." They agreed that until that time, he should visit her every evening, for the old witch always came in the day.

The old witch suspected nothing, until one day Rapunzel wondered aloud, "Why are you so much heavier to pull up than the prince? He is up in a moment."

"You wicked child!" screeched the witch. "What did you say? I thought I had shut you away from the world, but you have tricked me!" She was so angry that she took a pair of scissors and cut off all Rapunzel's beautiful hair. *Snip-snap* went the scissors, and the lovely tresses fell to the floor. Then the pitiless witch sent Rapunzel into the desert to live in grief and want.

That evening, the witch fastened the severed tresses to the window latch, and when the prince called,

> *Rapunzel, Rapunzel,*
> *Let down your hair,*

she let the hair down. The prince climbed up, but instead of his dear Rapunzel he found the witch, who fixed him with her evil eyes.

"Ah!" she said. "Your lovebird has flown. She is no longer singing in her nest. And she won't be singing anymore. The cat has taken her, and she'll scratch your eyes out too. You've lost Rapunzel. You'll never see her again."

The prince was in an agony of grief. In despair he leaped from the tower. His fall was broken by brambles, but the thorns scratched his eyes and left him blind.

The prince wandered blindly through the forest, living on roots and berries, and weeping and wailing over the loss of his dear wife.

He wandered in misery like this for several years, until at last he came to the desert where Rapunzel was living a wretched existence with the twins she had borne—a boy and a girl. He heard a voice that seemed familiar, and approached it. Rapunzel recognized him at once and flung herself weeping around his neck.

Two of Rapunzel's tears fell on his eyes, and gave him back his sight.

He took her back to his kingdom. They were welcomed with great rejoicing and lived happily together for many years to come.

CLEVER ELSIE

There was once a man who had a daughter who was known as Clever Elsie. A young man heard about her, and thought, *I don't have much in the way of brains myself, so she's the girl for me.* His name was Hans.

He said to Elsie's dad, "I want to marry her, but only if she's really smart. Common or garden bright won't do. I want a real clever-clogs."

"Never you worry," said Dad. "My Elsie is so clever it makes my brain hurt just to think of it. She can see the wind coming up the street and hear flies cough."

So they sat down to discuss the match over a meal. But the drink ran out. "Elsie," said Dad, "pop down to the cellar and fetch some more beer."

So Elsie took a jug and went down to the cellar. Well, that was a bit boring, so she amused herself by flipping up the lid and banging it down again as she walked. When she got to the barrel, the barrel was too high, so she stood on a chair to avoid hurting her back. You can't be too careful about these things.

Standing on the chair, she saw that there was an old pickaxe hanging on the wall right above the barrel. And she started to think.

What if I marry Hans, and we have a son, and he grows up, and we send him down to the cellar to draw beer, and a pickaxe falls on his head? It would kill him for sure! And she started to weep at the cruelty of it all. She got off the chair, lay down on the floor, and howled.

Well, upstairs they were worried so they sent the maid to see what was up. The maid said, "What's to-do? Why are you crying?"

"Why am I crying?" said Elsie. "Who wouldn't cry, with my terrible luck? If I marry Hans, and we have a son and send him down to the cellar to draw beer, a pickaxe may fall on his head and kill him! Boo-hoo!"

And the maid thought, *How clever Elsie is!* and she started to cry too.

Then the manservant went down to see what was up, and when he heard Elsie's sad story, he started crying too. Then Elsie's mother went down, and then Elsie's father, and soon they were both in floods of tears too.

At last Hans himself went down. "Whatever's the matter?" he asked.

"Ah, my dear," said Elsie, "life is hard. If we marry and have a son and send him down to the cellar to draw beer, a pickaxe may fall on his head and kill him."

Hans had never heard of anyone who thought as deeply as that.

"I don't need any more proofs of your cleverness," he said. "I'll marry you today!"

After they had been married awhile, Hans said, "I must go out to work to earn money. While I am gone, you cut the corn so that we can have flour for our bread."

When Hans was gone, Elsie made herself some porridge to take out into the field, in case she felt hungry.

When she got to the field, she was hungry already. "What shall I do?" she asked herself. "Cut first or eat first?" And she decided to eat first.

When she had eaten, Elsie felt sleepy. "What shall I do?" she asked herself. "Cut first or sleep first?" And she decided to sleep first.

When Hans came home that evening, Elsie was still not back. How clever she is, he thought. *She doesn't leave the field until the job is finished.* He went to join her, and found her fast asleep and the corn uncut.

Hans couldn't think how to wake her, but then he had a bright idea. He went back home and brought a net of the kind they use to catch birds, with lots of little bells on it, and threw it over Elsie. But she didn't wake. So he gave up and went home, locked the door, and sat down to his supper.

It was quite dark when Elsie woke, tangled in the net that chimed whenever she moved. She couldn't work out where she was, or even who she was. "I thought I was Clever Elsie," she said, "but Clever Elsie doesn't jingle when she moves. Am I or aren't I?"

There was only one way to find out. She went to Elsie and

Hans's house and knocked at the door. "Hans," she shouted, "is Elsie in?"

"Yes," said Hans, not thinking. "She's here."

"Oh my fingers and toes!" she cried. "Then I'm not me!"

She ran off through the village, jingling and chiming as she went, and no one has seen her since.

HANS THE HEDGEHOG

There was once a farmer who had plenty of money and land, but he was unhappy, because he had no children. Once when he went to town, the other farmers mocked him, so when he got home he said in a temper, "I must have a child, even if it's only a hedgehog."

So when his wife had a son, he was half human, half hedgehog. His little legs were all right, but he was a hedgehog from the waist up. The mother was frightened. She couldn't even nurse him, because he was so spiky. She said, "Look what trouble your temper has got us into now."

But the farmer said, "There's no use crying over spilt milk. What shall we call the boy?"

And the wife said, "There's only one name for him: Hans the Hedgehog."

"Where shall he sleep?"

"We can't put him in a proper bed, because of his quills." So

they strewed some handfuls of straw behind the stove, and that was his bed for the next eight years.

By that time his father was sick of him, and only wished he would die. But he didn't die, he just lay there behind the stove.

One day the farmer went to the fair and asked his wife what she would like him to buy her. "A joint of meat and some white bread rolls," she said. Then he asked the servant, and she said, "A pair of slippers and some fancy stockings." And finally he asked Hans the Hedgehog, and Hans answered, "Bring me some bagpipes, if you please."

When he returned from the fair he gave his wife the meat and the rolls, and the servant the slippers and the stockings. Lastly he went to the stove and gave the bagpipes to Hans the Hedgehog. Then Hans said, "Father, please go to the forge and have the rooster shod. Then I'll ride away and never come back."

The father thought the loss of his rooster well worth it to get rid of Hans the Hedgehog, so he took it to the forge to be shod. When it was done, Hans mounted the rooster and rode away, with his bagpipes under his arm. But he took all the farmer's pigs with him, which the farmer hadn't bargained on.

Hans the Hedgehog went to live in the forest and tend his herd of pigs, which soon grew very large. The rooster sat on a branch of a tall tree, with Hans on its back, and Hans practiced his bagpipes until the music he got out of them was really beautiful. All this time, his father and mother had no idea what he was doing.

One day, the king got lost in the forest and heard the music.

He sent a servant to find out what it was, and when the man returned he said, "Your Majesty, it is a hedgehog mounted on a rooster perched up a tall tree, playing the bagpipes."

The king was very curious and went to see Hans for himself and ask if he knew the way to the palace. So Hans came down from the tree and said, "I will show you the way if you will give me the first living creature you meet when we reach the palace courtyard."

The king took pen and paper and wrote something down and gave the paper to Hans, saying, "There, you have my written word on it." But he had written that Hans should not have the first thing he saw, for he thought, *He's only a dumb hedgehog, and I can write what I like.*

When he reached the palace, the first living creature the king saw was his daughter, running out to greet him. He told her what a joke it was that he had promised to give the first living creature he saw to the strange hedgehog who rode a rooster and played the bagpipes. "But don't worry," he said, "the promise isn't worth the paper it's not written on."

"That's just as well," said the princess, "for I wouldn't have gone with him, anyway."

Meanwhile Hans the Hedgehog lived happily in the forest, tending his pigs and playing his bagpipes.

It happened that another king got lost in the forest and made the same bargain with Hans in order to be shown the way home. But this king was an honest man. When his only daughter came running to greet him, he told her, "I was lost in the forest, and in order to find the way home, I promised to give the first living creature I met when I got back to a strange creature, half man and half hedgehog, who was sitting on a rooster in a tall tree, playing the bagpipes. I'm sorry, my dear, but that first living creature is you."

The brave girl said, "Never mind, Father. A promise is a promise, and I will go with him willingly if he comes to claim me."

After a while, Hans the Hedgehog had so many pigs that there wasn't room for them all in the forest, so he decided to go home. He sent word to his father that he was coming, with enough pigs for everyone in the village to have one. But his father wasn't pleased to see him, for he had hoped that Hans the Hedgehog had died years ago. So Hans said, "Father, take the rooster back to the forge and have him shod again, and I will ride away and never come back as long as I live." So his father took the rooster to be shod, and Hans rode away on him.

Hans rode to the kingdom of the first king. The king had given orders that if ever anyone came mounted on a rooster and playing the bagpipes, the army must kill him. So as soon as Hans appeared he was attacked from all sides. But he spurred on the rooster, and it rose into the air, right over the palace gates, to the king's window, and landed on the window ledge.

"Give me what you promised," said Hans the Hedgehog, "or I'll kill you and your daughter too."

The king was so frightened, he begged his daughter to save them by going out to Hans the Hedgehog. So she dressed herself in white, and her father gave her a carriage with six horses, and servants and a rich dowry. She got into the carriage, and Hans the Hedgehog got in beside her with his rooster and his bagpipes, and they drove away. The king thought he would never see his daughter again; but at least his own skin was safe.

They hadn't gone far when Hans the Hedgehog asked the princess, "Will you love me truly?"

"Yes," she said. But when he tried to kiss her, she turned away. His spikes caught her across the face, and left a smear of blood.

"You are false at heart," said Hans the Hedgehog. "Go home to your father, I don't want you." And no one else ever wanted her either.

Then Hans the Hedgehog rode on to the kingdom of the second king. This king had given orders that if anyone came riding a rooster and playing the bagpipes, he should be saluted, and brought to the palace at once.

When the king's daughter saw him she was frightened, for he did look very strange. But she told herself that it was wrong to judge people on appearances, and that anyway, a promise was a promise. So she welcomed Hans the Hedgehog with open arms, and they were married.

After the wedding feast, they went up to their room. She was still frightened, but Hans said, "Don't be afraid. I would never hurt you." Then he said to the king, "Tell four men to watch outside the bedroom door. When I go to bed I shall tear off my hedgehog's skin and cast it to the floor. They must rush in and throw it onto the fire, and watch until it is utterly devoured by the flames. Then I shall be free from the enchantment of my birth."

The men did as they were told, and when the skin was quite

burnt up, Hans lay in the bed in human form, as shapely and handsome as could be. The king's daughter loved him truly, and the king named him his heir.

My tale it is done,
Away it has run
From my house to your house
To sit in the sun.

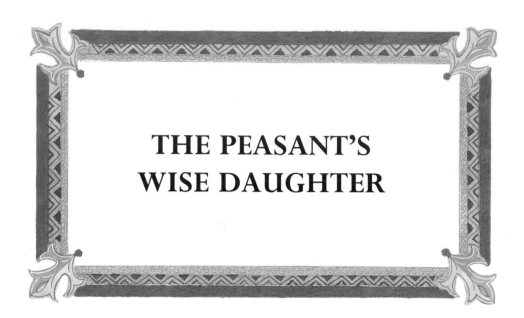

THE PEASANT'S
WISE DAUGHTER

There was once a poor peasant who had no land, just a little hut and an only daughter.

One day the daughter said, "We ought to ask the king for a piece of newly cleared land."

When the king heard how poor they were, he gave them a piece of land, which the girl and her father dug over, meaning to sow it with corn and wheat. When they had turned over nearly the whole field, they dug up a mortar made of pure gold.

"Look here," said the father. "As the king was so kind as to give us this field, we ought to give him the golden mortar in return."

The daughter was dead against it. "Father," she said, "if we give the king the golden mortar, he will the demand a golden pestle to go with it, and then what shall we do?" But the old man wouldn't listen.

He took the mortar and presented it to the king. But instead of saying thank you, the king just said, "Are you sure that's all you found?"

"Yes, Your Majesty," said the peasant.

"I don't believe you," said the king. "If you found a golden mortar, you must have found a golden pestle. Bring it to me, or you shall regret it."

The old man protested that he had never seen the golden pestle, but he might as well have saved his breath to cool his porridge. They dragged him off to prison, where he was to stay until he produced the pestle.

The guards who brought him his bread and water couldn't persuade him to eat or drink. All he did was wail, "If only I had listened to my daughter!" They reported this to the king, and the king had the peasant brought before him.

"What do you mean, 'If only I had listened to my daughter'?" asked the king.

"She told me not to give you that mortar, as you would only ask for the pestle as well."

"If you have such a wise daughter, send her to me."

So the peasant's daughter had to appear before the king. He said, "If you are as wise as you seem, I shall marry you. But first you must solve a riddle."

"I will try," said the girl.

The king said, "I want you to come to me neither naked nor clothed, neither riding nor walking, and neither on the road nor off the road. If you can do that, you shall be my queen."

The peasant girl went home and took off all her clothes. Then she wrapped herself in a fishing net, so that she was not naked.

Then she hired a donkey and tied the fishing net to the donkey's tail, so that it could pull her along, which was neither riding nor walking. As the donkey pulled her along, it dragged her through the wagon ruts, with only her big toe touching the road. So she was neither on the road nor off the road.

When the king saw the clever way in which she had solved his riddle, he released her father from prison, took her as his wife, and put her in charge of his household.

Some years passed, and then one day as the king was inspecting his troops it happened that two peasants who had been selling wood stopped their wagons outside the palace. One wagon was drawn by two oxen, and the other by two horses. One of the horses had a young foal with it, and this foal ran off and lay down between the oxen. When the foal's owner asked for it back, the other peasant refused, and the two came to blows.

The king wanted to know what the matter was, and the peasants argued their case in front of him. "The foal is mine," said the peasant with the horses. "Nonsense," said the other. "The foal is mine. See how happy it is, lying down between its parents." And the king, who knew nothing about animals, said, "The creature seems happy where it is, so that's where it should stay."

The peasant who had lost his foal didn't dare argue with the king, but he had heard that the queen was kindhearted and came from a peasant family herself, so he took his troubles to her. "Please help me," he begged.

"I will," she said, "if you promise never to betray me. This is what you must do. Tomorrow morning, when the king goes out to inspect the guard, you must stand in the middle of the road with a fishing net and pretend to be fishing in the dust. Every now and then give the net a shake as if it were full, and then carry on." And she also told him what to say when the king spoke to him.

Next day, the king asked him what he thought he was up to. "I'm fishing," he replied.

"How can you catch fish on dry land?" asked the king.

"There's just as much chance of my catching fish on dry land as there is of oxen having a foal."

"You didn't fetch that answer out of your own head," said the king. "Who told you what to say?" But the peasant, because he had promised the queen, would not betray her. The king had him dragged off to prison and beaten and starved until at last he confessed that it was the queen who had advised him what to do and say.

When the king got home, he said to his wife, "You have made me a laughingstock. I won't have you for my wife anymore. You can go back to the peasant's hut you came from." He only granted her one mercy—that she could take with her whatever was dearest to her as a farewell gift.

The queen replied with downcast eyes, "Of course, my husband, if that is your will." She threw her arms around him and kissed him and begged him to drink one last drink with her.

The king didn't know that his drink contained a strong sleeping potion. No sooner had he drunk it than he was fast asleep.

The queen took a fine white sheet and wrapped the king in it, and carried him out to a carriage. Then she drove to the old hut that belonged to her father and laid the king in her own old bed.

The king slept a whole day and night without waking. When he finally came to, he had no idea where he was or what had happened. He called for his servants, but there were no servants. At last his wife came to his side. She said, "My husband, you told me I could take from the palace whatever was dearest to me, so I did. I took you, for you are more precious to me than the whole world."

The king's eyes filled with tears. "My dearest wife," he said. "You are as wise as ever. You shall be mine, and I shall be yours." And he took her back to the palace, and never parted from her again.

THE MILLER'S BOY
AND THE CAT

There was an old miller who lived in a mill with no wife or child but only three lads who worked for him. After some years, he said, "I'm getting old. All I want to do is sit by the fire. So I've decided to give the mill to one of you. Whoever brings me back the finest horse shall have the mill, so long as he looks after me until I die."

Now two of the boys were sharp enough, but the third was a nincompoop. The other boys made fun of him and said, "What would you do with a mill, stupid?" And he wasn't even sure himself if he would want it.

The three of them set out together, but when they got to a village, the first two told stupid Hans, "You might as well stop here. You'll never get a horse as long as you live." But Hans stayed with them. At nightfall they came to a cave in which they lay down to sleep, but the two smart ones just waited until Hans had dropped off and then sneaked away, leaving him behind.

They thought that was very funny—though, as it turned out, the joke was on them.

When the sun rose, Hans woke to find himself alone in the deep cave. He looked around him, and exclaimed, "Heavens, where am I?" He got up, clambered out of the cave, and found himself in the forest. "I'm lost and alone. How will I ever find a horse now?" he moaned.

As he walked along, thinking such thoughts, a little tabby cat came up to him, and said in a friendly way, "'Morning, Hans. What can I do for you?"

"I'm afraid you can't help me," said Hans.

"I know what you're looking for," the cat replied. "You're looking for a fine horse. Well, if you'll come with me and do my bidding for seven years, I will give you the finest horse you ever laid eyes on."

This is a peculiar cat, thought Hans. *I wonder if she's telling the truth*. There was only one way to find out, so Hans agreed to serve the cat for seven years.

The cat took him back to her enchanted castle. All the servants were kittens, who bounded upstairs and downstairs all day, always happy and playful.

In the evening, when Hans and the tabby cat sat down to dinner, three of the kittens made music for them. One played the double bass, another the fiddle, while the third puffed and blew on a trumpet. And after dinner, the tabby cat said, "Hans, will you dance with me?"

Hans said, "No. I've never danced with a pussycat, and I never will."

So the cat told the kittens to show Hans to his room. One of them showed the way with a candle, another took his shoes off, another took his stockings off, and another blew out the light. And in the morning they came back and helped him get dressed. One put his stockings on for him, another tied his garters, one brought his shoes, one washed him, and another dried his face with her tail. "How soft that is!" he said.

But Hans had his own work to do. Every day he had to chop wood with a silver axe and a silver saw, a copper mallet and silver wedges.

All the time Hans was in the castle he was very well fed and looked after, but he never saw a soul other than the tabby cat and the kittens.

One day, the cat asked Hans to go and mow the meadow and bring in the hay. She gave him a silver scythe and a gold whetstone, and he set to work. When the haymaking was done, Hans said, "Isn't it time for my reward?"

"You must do one more thing for me first. I want you to build me a little house. Here is everything you need—wood, and tools all of silver."

Hans built the little house, and when he was finished he said, "Now I have done everything you asked, but I still have no horse." The seven years had flown by like so many months.

"Would you like to see my horses?" asked the tabby cat.

"Yes!" said Hans.

So the cat opened the door of the little silver house that Hans had built, and inside there stood twelve horses, so sleek and glossy that his heart jumped for joy. Then the cat gave Hans food and drink, and said, "I will not give you your horse yet. You go home, and I will follow in three days."

The cat showed him the way to the mill, and Hans set out. Now the cat had never given him any new clothes, so he was still in the same old smock he had come in; and after seven years it was dirty and torn, and far too small.

When he reached the mill, the two smart lads were already there, and each of them had brought a horse, though one of the horses was blind and the other was lame. "Where's your horse, stupid?" they crowed.

"It will follow me in three days," he replied, and they fell about laughing.

The miller wouldn't even let Hans come inside, because he was so ragged and filthy. "What if we have guests?" the miller said. "You'd put us to shame." So Hans had to eat on the doorstep, and sleep in the goosehouse on the hard straw.

When he woke up in the morning, the three days had passed. A coach came to the mill, drawn by six shining horses, and a servant was leading a seventh horse, which was for the miller's boy. A beautiful princess stepped out of the coach and went into the mill, and this princess was the tabby cat Hans had served for seven years.

She asked the miller, "Do you have a boy who serves you?"

"Two of the rascals," said the miller, pointing to the two smart lads.

"Isn't there another?"

"Oh, him!" the miller replied. "He's too dirty to come in here; he's in the goosehouse."

"Bring him to me," said the princess. So they fetched him from the goosehouse. He was holding his tattered smock together for modesty's sake. But the princess's servants unpacked splendid clothes for him. They washed him and dressed him, and when they were finished, he looked as handsome as any king.

Then the princess said, "Let me see the horses the other boys brought home." They showed her the blind nag and the lame one. Then the princess told her servants to bring forward the horse that they had brought for Hans. Its coat glistened, and its muscles rippled underneath its skin. When the miller saw it he said, "This is the finest horse that has ever entered this yard."

"That horse belongs to Hans," said the princess.

"Then so does the mill," said the miller.

But Hans didn't want the mill now. "You keep it," he said, "and the horse too."

Hans and the princess drove off in the coach and six, and went to live in the little silver house that he had built—only now it was a big castle, and everything in it was made of gold and silver. They were married, and Hans was so rich that he never had to work again.

Which just goes to show that even a nincompoop can get on in the world.

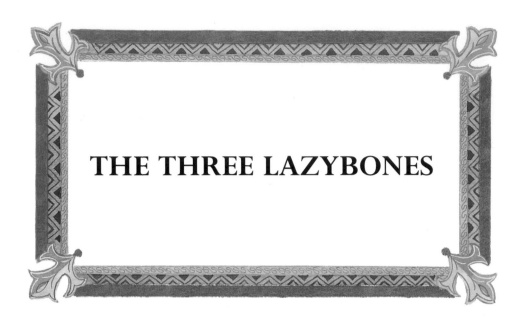

THE THREE LAZYBONES

Once there was a king who had three sons, whom he loved equally. He just couldn't decide which one should succeed him.

When he was lying on his deathbed, he called them to him. "The best kind of king is the kind that does nothing at all," he said. "Therefore I shall give the crown to whichever of you is the laziest."

The eldest said, "Then the kingdom is mine! I'm so lazy that if a raindrop falls in my eye, I can't summon up the energy to blink it out."

The second said, "No, the kingdom is mine! I am so idle that when I warm myself by the fire, I would rather let my foot burn than move my leg."

But the third said, "You two decide it among yourselves. It's just too much trouble to compete. All I know is that if I were going to be hanged and had the rope already around my neck, and someone handed me a sharp knife, I'd sooner let them hang me than raise my hand to cut the rope."

When the father heard that, he said, "You're the laziest of the lot. You shall be king."

THE GOLD CHILDREN

There were once a poor man and woman who had nothing but a little hut. They fished for their living and lived from hand to mouth.

One day the man cast his net and caught a fish that was all of gold.

As the man gaped down at his catch, the fish said, "Throw me back into the water, and I will change your hut into a castle."

"What use is a castle if I have nothing to eat?" the fisherman replied.

The gold fish told him, "In the castle there will be a cupboard which, whenever you open it, will be full of wonderful food."

"In that case," said the fisherman, "we have a deal."

"There is just one condition," said the fish. "If you tell anyone where your good luck has come from, you will lose every-thing."

The man threw the gold fish back into the water. When he got home, his hut was transformed into a magnificent castle, and his wife was dressed like a queen. "Husband," she said. "Look what's happened! I like it!"

"Me too," he said.

"But we still don't have anything to eat."

"Don't worry about that," said the husband, and he opened the cupboard that was indeed full of wonderful food.

"What more could the heart desire?" said the wife. "But where has it all come from?"

"Don't ask me that," he replied. "If I tell you, we'll lose it all."

"Well, if you don't want to tell me, that's all right," she said. But she didn't mean it. She couldn't rest until she knew. She pestered the poor man day and night until he told her about the gold fish. But as soon as the secret was out of his mouth, the castle disappeared, and they were back in their old hut again.

The husband had to go back to fishing for a living. But as luck would have it, he caught the gold fish again. He made the same deal as last time, and when he got home the castle was back. But once again his wife nagged him until he told her what had happened, and once again they lost everything.

The man went fishing once again, and for a third time he caught the gold fish.

"I can see that it is my fate to fall into your hands," said the fish. "Take me home and cut me in six pieces. Give your wife two of them to eat, give two to your horse, and bury two in the garden, and they will bring a blessing."

The fisherman did as he was told. From the two pieces he

buried in the ground sprang two golden lilies; the horse had two golden foals; and his wife gave birth to two boys with bodies of gold.

The boys grew tall and handsome, and the lilies and the horses grew with them. One day the boys said, "Father, we want to ride out into the world on our golden horses."

He was sad, and said, "But how will I bear it? I won't know how you are."

They answered, "As long as the golden lilies stand tall, all is well with us. But if they droop and fade, we shall be ill. If they wither, we shall be dead."

They rode off and came to an inn full of people who laughed and jeered at the gold children. Hearing their mockery, one of the boys was so ashamed that he didn't want to go on; he turned his horse around and rode home to his father and mother. But the other boy carried on.

He reached the edge of a great forest. The people there warned him, "Don't go into the forest. It's full of robbers. When they see that you and your horse are made of gold, they will kill you."

But he would not be frightened off. He took bearskins, such as tramps wore in those days, and covered himself and his horse with them, so that the gold could not be seen. He set off into the forest. Before long he heard voices. One said, "Here comes someone." The other replied, "It's only a tramp. Let him go; he looks as poor as a churchmouse." So the gold child rode through the forest and nothing harmed him.

One day he came to a village, where he saw a girl so beautiful

that he thought there could not be anyone more beautiful on earth. His love was so strong that he went up to her and said, "I love you with all my heart. Will you marry me?"

She liked the look of him just as much, and she answered, "Yes, I will be your wife and be true to you my whole life long."

Just as the priest was making them man and wife, her father came home. He was very suprised to find his daughter getting married. "Who's the bridegroom?" he asked, and the gold child was pointed out, still wrapped in his bearskins.

The father said angrily, "No tramp is going to marry my daughter!" He wanted to kill him.

But the bride begged for his life, saying, "He is my husband, and I love him with all my heart." And in the end her father calmed down.

Still, he wasn't happy. The next morning he got up early to take a look at the man and see if he really was just a common tramp. When he looked into the room, he saw a magnificent golden man lying sprawled across the bed. The cast-off bearskins were tumbled on the floor. *What a lucky escape!* he thought. *In my anger I might have committed a terrible crime.*

That night the gold child dreamed that he was hunting a splendid stag, and when he woke he told his wife, "I must go hunting."

She was worried and begged him to stay, saying, "I'm afraid something bad will happen to you." But he would not be dissuaded.

He went into the forest, and it wasn't long before a fine stag

appeared just as in his dream. He aimed, and was about to shoot, but the stag ran away. He chased it all day, over hedges and ditches, without ever catching it. In the evening, he lost its track.

There was a cottage nearby. It was a witch's house. The gold child knocked at the door, and the witch answered. "What are you doing in the forest so late in the day?"

"Have you seen a stag?"

"Oh yes, I know the stag well," she said.

Then a little dog came out of the cottage and started barking ferociously at the gold child.

"Be quiet, you beast, or I'll shoot you," he said.

"What?" cried the witch in a temper. "Would you kill my dog?" She turned him to stone, and he toppled to the ground.

His bride waited in vain for him to come home. She thought, *The bad thing I dreaded has come to pass.*

Back at home, the other gold brother was standing beside the gold lilies when one of them suddenly drooped. "Something terrible has happened to my brother!" he said. "I must go to his aid."

The father begged him to stay at home. "What if I lose you too?"

But he said, "I must go, and I will."

He mounted his gold horse and rode into the forest where his brother was lying, turned to stone. The old witch came out of her cottage and called to him. She wanted to turn him to stone too. But he was too clever for her. He did not go near her, but shouted, "Bring my brother back to life, or I will shoot you."

The witch didn't want to, but she touched the stone with her finger, and it came back to life.

The two gold children hugged each other and kissed. They were full of joy. Then they rode out of the forest, one home to his bride, the other to their father. The father said, "I knew the moment you saved your brother, for the gold lily suddenly stood up as fresh and straight as ever."

They all lived happily their whole lives long.

THE MUSICIANS OF BREMEN

A man had a donkey that served him faithfully for many a long year, hauling sacks of grain to the mill. But at last the donkey's strength began to fail; the work was getting too much for him.

Then the master began to complain about the cost of the donkey's keep, and the donkey, seeing which way the wind was blowing, ran away along the road to Bremen, thinking he might be able to join the town band.

When he had gone some little way he found a dog lying by the road, panting as if he had just run a race.

"Hey-up, shaggy," said the donkey. "What's your problem?"

"Because I am old and can no longer hunt, my master decided to have me put down, so I ran away. But I am weak, so how am I to earn a living?"

"Come with me to Bremen to join the band," said the donkey. "I'll play the lute, and you'll play the drum." The dog perked up at that idea, and the two went along together.

It wasn't long before they saw a cat sitting by the road with a face like a wet week.

"Hey-up, whiskers," said the donkey. "Why so sad?"

"Who can be happy when their life is threatened?" replied the cat. "Just because I am getting old, and my teeth are worn down, my mistress wanted to drown me; so I ran away. But what am I to do now? At my age, I should be sitting by the fire, not out hunting for my supper."

"Come to Bremen with us. You're a born singer, so you can join the band with us." The cat liked the idea, so she went along.

Soon the three runaways came to a farmyard. The rooster was sitting on the gate, crowing at the top of his voice.

"Oh, that sound!" said the donkey. "It sets your teeth on edge. Why are you making such a racket?"

"I'm foretelling good weather, for it's the day Our Lady washes the Christ Child's shirts, so it's bound to be fine drying weather. But it's not so good for me, for tomorrow's Sunday, and we have guests, and I heard the farmer's wife tell the cook to wring my neck tonight and serve me up as soup tomorrow. She has no pity. That's why I'm crowing now, while I still can."

"Red-comb, don't be a fool. Come with us to Bremen. Whatever happens, it's bound to be better than death. You've got a strong voice; maybe if we all sing together we'll really make music!"

The rooster agreed, and the four went on together down the road to Bremen. They could not reach the city before nightfall, so they spent that night in the forest. The donkey and the dog

settled down under a big tree, the cat climbed up on a branch, and the rooster flew to the top of the tree, where he felt safest. Before going to sleep, he looked around in every direction. He thought he saw a spark in the distance and told his companions that there must be a house nearby, for he had seen a light.

"In that case," said the donkey, "let's go there, for I can't get comfortable under this tree."

The dog agreed. "Where there's a house, there are usually bones," he said, "and bones aren't bad."

So they set off in the direction of the light. It grew brighter and brighter, until at last they came to a house. It was the house of a gang of robbers.

The donkey, who was the tallest, went to the lit window and peered in. "What can you see, long-ears?" asked the rooster.

"What can I see?" replied the donkey. "I can see a table covered with good things to eat and drink, and a gang of robbers sitting down and feasting at it."

"That's what we want," said the rooster.

"Oh, yes! If only!" said the donkey.

But how were they to drive the robbers away? The animals talked it over, and at last they came up with a plan.

The donkey stood with his forefeet on the window ledge. The dog jumped on the donkey's back. The cat climbed on top of the dog. The rooster flew up and landed on the cat's head.

Then they struck up the band. The donkey brayed, the dog barked, the cat meowed, and the rooster crowed. Then they leaped through the window and landed in the room in a shower of glass.

The robbers thought it must be a monster. They were so frightened that they fled into the forest, leaving the house for the animals, who settled themselves at the table and ate their fill.

When the four musicians could eat no more, they put out the light and found themselves places to sleep. The donkey lay down on the dung heap in the yard. The dog lay by the back door. The cat curled up on the warm ashes in the hearth. And the rooster perched up on top of the roof. Being tired out from their long walk, they soon went to sleep.

When it was past midnight, the robbers saw from a distance that the light had gone out. They began to think they had been fools to be scared off so easily. The chief robber told one of the others to go and have a look-see.

The robber crept in through the front door. All was quiet, but it was too dark to see. He went to the fire to try to light a match. The cat opened her eyes, and the robber, thinking they were burning embers, held the match up to them.

The cat didn't think this was funny. She sprang at the robber's face, spitting and scratching.

Scared to bits, the robber ran to the back door, but the dog jumped up and bit him in the leg.

The robber stumbled out into the yard, but as he passed the dung heap the donkey kicked him with his strong hind legs.

The rooster, who had been woken by all the commotion, started crowing from the roof, "What-a-to-do! What-a-to-do!"

At that the robber ran back as fast as he could to his fellows and said, "There's a horrible witch in the house, who spat at me and scratched my face with her long claws. Behind the door, there's a man with a knife, who stabbed me in the leg. In the yard, there's a huge monster who hit me on the head with a wooden club. And above them all, sitting on the roof, is a judge, who called out, 'The jailhouse for you! The jailhouse for you!' I only just made it out by the skin of my teeth."

The robbers never dared go near the house again, and as the four musicians liked it so well, they never left it. And the mouth of the last person who told this story is still warm.

RUMPELSTILTSKIN

Once there was a miller who was very poor but had a beautiful daughter. One day he happened to be talking to the king and, to puff himself up, he said, "My daughter can spin straw into gold."

The king said to the miller, "How fascinating! If your daughter is as clever as you say, bring her to the palace tomorrow, and we'll see what she can do."

When the girl was brought to him he took her into a room full of straw, gave her a spinning wheel, and said, "Off you go then! I'm sure you'll have spun all this straw into gold by tomorrow morning. But if you haven't, you must die."

He locked her in the room and left her there alone.

The poor girl sat there, and for the life of her she didn't know what to do. She hadn't the first idea how to spin straw into gold. She was so terrified she began to cry.

All at once the door opened, and in stepped a little man.

"Good evening," he said. "Why are you crying so?"

"Oh," she said, "I'm supposed to spin straw into gold, and I don't know how."

"What will you give me if I spin it for you?"

"My necklace," said the girl.

The little man took the necklace, sat down at the wheel, and *whirr, whirr, whirr*, three turns, and the reel was full. Then he put on another, and *whirr, whirr, whirr*, three turns, and the second reel was full. All night he worked, and in the morning all the straw was spun and all the reels were full of gold.

The king came first thing in the morning, and when he saw the reels of gold he was delighted. His heart swelled with greed. He took the miller's daughter to a larger room full of straw and told her to spin this too into gold if she valued her life.

She didn't know what to do, and she was crying, when the door opened, and the little man appeared. He said, "What will you give me if I spin this straw into gold for you?"

"The ring from my finger."

The little man took the ring, sat down at the wheel, and by morning he had spun all the straw into glittering gold.

The king was full of joy at the sight; but still he didn't have enough gold. He took the girl to a still larger room full of straw and said, "You must spin this into gold tonight. If you succeed, you shall be my wife." He said to himself, *She may only be a miller's daughter, but I couldn't find a richer wife in the whole world.*

When the girl was alone, the little man came in for the third time, and said, "What will you give me if I spin the straw into gold for you this time?"

"I have nothing left to give," said the girl.

"Then promise me, if you should ever become queen, to give me your first child."

Who knows what life will bring? thought the girl. She had no choice but to promise the little man what he wanted, and for that he spun the straw into gold.

When the king came in the morning and found all as he wished, he married her, and the miller's pretty daughter became a queen.

A year later, she brought a beautiful baby into the world. She had forgotten all about the little man. But suddenly he came into her room, and said, "Now give me what you promised."

The queen was horror-struck. She offered him all the riches in the kingdom if he would let her keep the child. But the little man said, "A living soul is more precious to me than all the treasures in the world."

The queen wept so bitterly that the little man took pity on her. "I will give you three days' grace. If, in that time, you can find out my name, you may keep the child."

The queen tossed and turned all night, thinking of every name she had ever heard of, and she sent a messenger across the country to ask what other names there might be. When the little man came next day, she began with Caspar, Melchior, and Balthazar, and reeled off every name she knew, one after another; but to every one the little man said, "That is not my name."

On the second day she sent the messenger back out to ask for names, and she tried all the unusual ones on the little man.

"Is your name Sparerib, or Sheepshank, or Laceleg?"

But he always answered no.

On the third day the messenger told her, "As I walked at the edge of the forest, where the fox and the hare bid each other good night, I came to the foot of a mountain. There I saw a little hut, and outside the hut a fire was blazing. A funny little man was hopping around the fire, singing,

> *Today I brew, tomorrow bake,*
> *And after that the child I'll take.*
> *I'm the winner of the game,*
> *Rumpelstiltskin is my name."*

The queen was so glad to hear that!

Soon the little man arrived. He said, "Now, Your Majesty, what is my name?"

"Is it Tom?"

"No."

"Is it Dick?"

"No."

"Is it Harry?"

"No."

"Could it be . . . Rumpelstiltskin?"

"The devil told you that," the little man screamed. "The devil told you that!" He was so angry that he stamped his right foot so deep into the ground that his whole leg went in. Then in his rage he pulled his left foot so hard that he tore himself in two.

So the queen kept her baby, and loved it all the more because she had so nearly lost it.

MANYFURS

There was once a king who had a wife with golden hair. She was so beautiful that there was none on earth to compare with her. When she fell ill and knew that she must soon die, she called the king to her and said, "If you wish to marry again after my death, promise me that you won't take anyone who isn't as beautiful as me and who hasn't got golden hair like mine." And after the king had given his word, she closed her eyes and died.

For a long time the king grieved and had no thought of marrying again. But at last his councillors told him, "You must re-marry." For the king had no son, but only a daughter.

Messengers were sent far and wide looking for a bride who was as beautiful as the late queen and who had such golden hair, but there was no one. So the messengers came home empty-handed.

The only person who was as beautiful as the queen and who had such lovely golden hair was the king's own daughter. And

74

one day the king, who was really half out of his mind with grief and worry, said, "I shall marry my daughter."

The councillors told him that he must not. "God forbids it," they said. "No good would come from such a sin. You will drag the whole kingdom down to hell with you."

But the king was determined. "She is the only one who looks like my dear wife, so she is the one I should marry," he said.

The daughter was even more shocked when she heard of the plan, and decided she must hinder it. So she told him, "Before I consent to marry you, I must have three dresses, one as golden as the sun, one as silver as the moon, and one as bright and sparkling as the stars. Also, I must have a cloak made from a thousand different furs, and one of every kind of animal in the kingdom must give a piece of its skin for it." For she thought that the king would never be able to find such garments.

But the king set all the seamstresses and all the hunters in the kingdom to work, and at length all the garments were ready: three dresses, as golden as the stars, as silver as the moon, and as bright as the stars, and a cloak made of a thousand different furs.

As the king spread out the many-furred cloak he said, "Tomorrow shall be our wedding day."

When the princess saw that there was no hope of changing the king's mind, she resolved to run away. That night when everyone was asleep, she got up, and took three things from among her treasures—a golden ring, a tiny golden spinning wheel, and a tiny golden bobbin. Then she put her dresses of the sun, moon, and stars into a nutshell, put on her cloak of a thousand furs, rubbed dirt into her face and hands, and walked out into the forest, trusting to God to watch over her. She walked until she was exhausted, and then she curled up asleep in a hollow log.

The sun rose, but she went on sleeping. She was still asleep when the sun was high. Now it so happened that the king to whom this forest belonged was hunting in it. When his dogs came to the tree, they sniffed, and ran around the tree, barking. The king ordered his huntsman to see what wild beast was hiding there.

"It's a strange beast," the huntsman reported. "I've never seen its like. It is lying asleep in a hollow log, and its skin is covered with a thousand different furs."

The king said, "Try and catch it alive. Tie it to the wagon and take it home."

When the huntsman grabbed hold of the princess, she awoke with a start, and cried in terror, "Have pity on me! I'm a poor child, abandoned by my father and mother. Look after me."

He said, "Manyfurs, you can come and work in the kitchen. You can sweep up the ashes." And she was bundled into the wagon and taken back to the palace. She was given a hidey-hole under the stairs to sleep in, where the sun never shone, and told, "This is your place, Manyfurs." Then she was sent into the kitchen to do the heavy work. They made her carry wood and water, sweep the hearth, pluck the chickens, clean the vegetables, rake the ashes—all the dirty jobs.

Manyfurs lived a wretched life. Alas, fair princess, what's to become of you?

After a long time, a ball was given in the palace, and she asked the chef, "May I go upstairs and watch for a little while? I'll stay outside the door."

The chef said, "Yes, but you must be back in half an hour to sweep the hearth."

Manyfurs took her oil lamp into her hidey-hole, took off her cloak of a thousand furs, washed the grime off her face and hands, and let her beauty shine once more. Then she opened the nutshell and took out her dress as golden as the sun.

As she made her way up to the ballroom, everyone made way for her. No one recognized her. They thought she must be a princess. The king himself came up to her, took her hand, and danced with her. He thought in his heart, *This is the most beautiful girl in the world.*

When the dance ended, she curtsied. The king looked away for a moment, and when he looked back, she was gone. No one had seen her leave. The king had all the guards questioned, but no one knew where she had come from or where she had gone.

She had run into her hidey-hole, slipped out of her dress, rubbed dirt on her face and hands, put on her cloak of a thousand furs, and become Manyfurs again.

She went to the kitchen to sweep the hearth, but the chef said, "Never mind with that now. I want to see the dancing, so you make some soup for the king, and mind you don't drop any hairs in it or you'll get no supper."

The chef went upstairs, and Manyfurs made bread soup for the king as best she knew how. Then she fetched her golden ring from her hidey-hole and put it in the bowl.

When the ball was over, the king ate the soup, and he liked it very much. When he got to the bottom of the bowl, he found the golden ring and wondered how it had got there. So he sent for the chef.

The chef was terrified. "You must have let a hair fall into the soup," he said, "and if you have, you shall be beaten for it."

When he came before the king, the king asked him who made the soup.

"I did," he replied.

"That is not true," said the king. "Tonight's soup was different. It was much better than usual."

So the chef had to admit that it was Manyfurs who made the soup.

"Then send her to me," said the king.

When Manyfurs came, the king said, "Who are you?"

"I'm a poor girl abandoned by her father and mother," she replied.

"What's your position here?"

"I'm here for people to throw boots at."

The king produced the ring. "Where did this ring come from?"

"What would poor Manyfurs know about a ring like that?" she replied. So the king got nothing out of her and had to send her back to the kitchen.

After a while, the king threw another ball. As before, Manyfurs begged the chef for leave to look on. "Yes," he answered, "but be sure to be back in half an hour to make the king that bread soup he likes so much."

She nipped into her hidey-hole, threw off her cloak, washed, and opened the nutshell to take out the dress as silver as the moon.

She looked as lovely as could be. The king danced with her, but once more she managed to slip away without being noticed.

She turned herself into Manyfurs again and made the king his soup. This time she slipped her tiny golden spinning wheel into the bowl.

Once again, the king summoned the chef and asked who had made the soup, and once again he admitted, "Manyfurs." But the king could get nothing more out of her this time, just that her place was to have boots thrown at her and what would she know of a golden spinning wheel?

The king held a third ball, and it was just the same as before. Manyfurs begged to go and watch, and the chef let her, saying, "Be sure and come back in time to make the king's soup. I think you must be a witch, Manyfurs, and put a spell on your soup to make the king like it so much better than mine."

She put on the dress that glittered like the stars and went into the ballroom. Once more, the king danced with the beautiful girl and thought that she had never looked so radiant. And while they were dancing he managed, without her noticing, to slip the golden ring onto her finger.

Every time the music seemed to be stopping, the king signed to the musicians to keep going. But at last it came to an end, and though the king tried to hold on to her, the girl tore herself loose and sprang away so quickly that she vanished before his eyes.

She rushed to her hidey-hole. She didn't have time to take off her dress of stars, but just threw her fur cloak on top of it. And when she rubbed the dirt onto her face and hands, she missed the finger with the ring.

Then she went back to the kitchen as Manyfurs and cooked the king's soup. This time, she hid the tiny golden bobbin at the bottom of the bowl.

When the king found the bobbin, he sent for Manyfurs. Noticing her white finger with the ring on it, he grasped her by the hand and held her fast. When she tried to struggle free, her cloak slipped aside, revealing the dress as bright and sparkling as the stars. The king pulled the many-furred cloak aside, and her lovely hair came tumbling down in a shower of gold. She could conceal herself beneath her many-furred cloak no longer. She washed the dirt from her face and hands and stood there in her glory, more beautiful than anyone who has ever been seen on earth.

The king said, "You are my dear bride, and we shall never part." They were married that day, and they lived happily ever after.

MOTHER SNOW

There was a widow who had two daughters. One of them was pretty and hardworking, while the other was ugly and lazy. But she was much fonder of the ugly, lazy one, because she was her own daughter, so she made her pretty stepdaughter do all the hard work of the house. Every day the poor girl had to sit by a well on the roadside and spin until her fingers bled.

Now it happened that one day when she bled on the spindle she dipped it in the well to wash it clean. But she lost her grip, and the spindle fell to the bottom. She burst into tears and ran to tell her stepmother what had happened. The stepmother gave her a tongue-lashing, and said, "You dropped it, so you must fetch it back."

So the girl went back to the well. She was at her wits' end, and, not knowing what else to do, she cast herself into the well in pursuit of the spindle. She lost her senses, and when she came to she was in a delightful meadow. The sun was shining, and the meadow was starred with lovely flowers.

She crossed the meadow, and after a while she came to a baker's oven full of bread. The bread cried out,

> *Take me out,*
> *I'm done to a turn.*
> *Take me out*
> *Before I burn!*

So she picked up the bread shovel and took out the loaves one by one.

She went on and came to a tree groaning with apples, and it cried out,

> *Pick me now,*
> *My apples are ripe.*
> *Shake me, shake me*
> *With all your might!*

So she shook the tree, and the apples fell like rain. When there were none left on the tree, she piled them up, and went on her way.

Finally she came to a little house. An old women was peering out of the window, and she had such big teeth that the girl was frightened and almost ran away. But the old woman called out to her, "There's nothing to be scared of. Stay with me and do my housework. If you serve me well, you won't regret it. Just take care to make my bed well, and shake it till the feathers fly—for then it will snow on earth. I am Mother Snow."

As the old woman spoke so kindly, the girl took heart and

agreed to stay with her. She did her work well and always shook the bed so hard that the feathers flew about like snowflakes. It was a pleasant life. The old woman never scolded her, and there were roasts or stews to eat every day.

Nevertheless, after a time the girl grew sad. At first she didn't know what was wrong, but then she realized she was homesick. Even though she was a thousand times better off here than at home, still she longed to go back. At last she said to the old woman, "I'm homesick. Although it's so nice here, I can't stay. I must go home."

Mother Snow said, "I'm glad you love your home. As you've served me so well, I shall take you there myself." Then she took the girl by the hand and led her to a doorway. The door was open, and as the girl went through a shower of gold fell on her, and covered her from head to toe. "That's your reward for your service," said Mother Snow. And then she gave the girl back the spindle she had dropped down the well.

When the door closed behind her, the girl was back on the earth again, not far from home. As she entered the yard, the rooster that was sitting on the well crowed,

> *Cock-a-doodle-doodle-doo!*
> *Our golden girl's come home—*
> *It's true!*

Then she went inside, and because she was covered in gold, her stepmother and sister made her welcome.

She told them everything that had happened, and when the mother heard how she had come by such wealth, she thought that

the ugly, lazy daughter deserved the same. So she told her to sit by the well and spin until her fingers bled. But the girl just stuck her hand in a thorn bush to prick it, threw the spindle in the well, and jumped in after it.

She woke in the same beautiful meadow as her sister, and took the same path across it. When she came to the bread oven, the bread cried out,

> *Take me out,*
> *I'm done to a turn.*
> *Take me out*
> *Before I burn!*

But the lazy girl answered, "Why should I get all dirty for you?" and walked on.

Soon she came to the apple tree, which cried,

> *Pick me now,*
> *My apples are ripe.*
> *Shake me, shake me*
> *With all your might.*

But she answered, "Shake yourself! An apple might fall on my head," and walked on.

When she arrived at Mother Snow's house she wasn't afraid, for she had been warned about the big teeth, so she agreed right away to work for her.

The first day she made the effort to work hard and do everything Mother Snow asked of her; the thought of all that money kept her going. But the second day she eased up, and the third day she barely lifted a finger, and after that she didn't bother to get up at all. She didn't even make Mother Snow's bed properly, and didn't shake it till the feathers flew.

Soon Mother Snow had had enough of her slovenly ways, and sent her packing. The girl was glad enough to go, for she was eager to get her share of gold. Mother Snow led her to the doorway, but as she passed though, a cauldron of sticky tar emptied itself over her. "That's your reward for your service," said Mother Snow, and shut the door.

So the lazy girl went home, all dripping with tar. When the rooster on the rim of the well saw her he crowed,

> *Cock-a-doodle-doodle-doo!*
> *Our dirty girl's come home—*
> *It's true!*

And the tar wouldn't come off. It stuck to her as long as she lived.

THE GOLDEN GOOSE

There was once a man who had three sons. The youngest of them was called Dimwit, and the others were always mocking him and never missed a chance to put him down.

One day the eldest son went into the forest to cut wood. His mother gave him a cake and a bottle of wine to keep him going.

When he reached the forest, he met a little old white-haired man, who said, "Good day to you. I'm hungry and thirsty. Give me a piece of your cake and a drink of your wine."

The clever son replied, "What I give to you, I take from myself. Be off with you!"

He started to cut down a tree, but it wasn't long before he missed his stroke and gashed open his arm, so that he had to go home and have it bandaged. That was the little old man's doing.

Then the second son went into the forest with a cake and a

bottle of wine that his mother gave him. He too met the little old white-haired man, who asked him to share his food and drink. But the second son replied cleverly, "If I give it to you, I won't have it for myself. Be off with you!"

He shouldn't have crossed the little old man. After only a few strokes at the tree, he cut himself in the leg and had to give up.

Then Dimwit said, "Father, let me go and cut wood."

The father replied, "Your brothers, who are clever, have tried it, and they have both hurt themselves. You know nothing, so you should leave it alone." But Dimwit begged and pleaded, and at last his father said, "If you hurt yourself, you'll just have to learn the hard way." His mother gave him a cake made of water and ashes, and a bottle of sour beer.

When he got to the forest, he too met the little old white-haired man, who greeted him and said, "Give me a piece of your cake and a drink from your bottle. I'm so hungry and thirsty."

Dimwit replied, "I've only got an ash cake and some sour beer, but you're welcome to share it."

So they sat down to eat, and when Dimwit brought out the cake, it was rich and sweet, and when he uncorked the bottle, the sour beer had turned into fine wine. So they ate and drank, and then the little old man said, "Because you have a good and generous heart, I will give you good luck. If you cut down that tree over there, you will find something in the roots. But don't take it home to your mean-hearted brothers." And with that the little old man went away.

Dimwit cut the tree down, and in its roots he found a goose

with feathers of pure gold. He picked it up in his arms, and carried it to a nearby inn, where he thought to stay the night. The innkeeper had three daughters, and when they saw the golden goose they were fascinated. They all wanted the golden feathers.

The eldest daughter thought, *I shall soon have a chance to pull out a feather*. When Dimwit went to bed, she grabbed hold of the bird's wing. As soon as she did so, her hand stuck fast.

The second daughter then came along with the same intention, but no sooner had she touched her sister's arm than she too was stuck like glue.

When the third daughter came, the two stuck sisters shouted, "Don't come near! Don't come near!" But she just thought they were trying to keep the golden goose for themselves, so she took no notice. As soon as she touched the second sister, she too was caught. So they had to spend the night stuck to the goose.

Next morning Dimwit picked up the goose in his arms and went on his way. He didn't trouble himself about the girls who were hanging on to it, and they had to keep up with him as best they could, running now left, now right, as the fancy took him.

When the parson saw them trotting this way and that across the fields, he called out, "For shame, you good-for-nothing girls! Running after a young man like that! Is that any way to behave?" And he caught hold of the youngest's hand. Then he too was stuck and had to run along with the others.

The sexton saw them running past, and called out, "Where are you going? Don't forget there is a christening today!" He ran

after them, and caught the parson by the sleeve, and then he was stuck too.

They called out to two peasants they passed, "Help us!" But as soon as the peasants touched the sexton, they too were stuck. So now there were seven of them running along behind Dimwit and the goose.

Later that day they came to a city where there was a king whose daughter was so solemn that she never laughed. The king had decreed that the first man who could make her laugh should marry her. When Dimwit heard that, he ran in front of her with the golden goose under his arm, and the seven stragglers running along behind.

When the princess saw the procession, she couldn't help herself. She began to laugh, and once she had started she could scarcely stop. So Dimwit said to the king, "Can I marry her now, then?"

The king was not very keen on Dimwit for a son-in-law, so he said, "Not quite yet. First, you must find a man who can drink my cellar dry."

Dimwit went back to the forest to look for the little old white-haired man. When he got to the place where he had felled the tree, he found a miserable-looking man sitting on the ground. "What's wrong?" asked Dimwit.

"I'm so thirsty!" said the man. "I can't abide cold water, and though I've just drunk a barrel of wine, that was no more use than a raindrop on a bonfire."

"I can help you there," said Dimwit. "Just come with me, and you shall quench your thirst." He led him to the king's cellar, and

the man set to work. He drank and drank until every barrel was dry, from the table wine to the rare vintages.

Dimwit went to the king, and said, "All the wine's gone. Can I marry her now?"

"Not quite yet," said the king. "First you must find a man who can eat all the bread in the palace bakery."

Dimwit went back to the forest, and in the place where he had felled the tree he found a man who was tightening a belt around his waist, with a look of terrible pain on his face. "What's wrong?" Dimwit asked.

"I'm so hungry!" the man replied. "Though I've eaten a whole ovenful of bread, that's like a crumb instead of a feast to a man with an appetite like mine. My stomach's empty."

"I can help you there," said Dimwit. "Come with me, and you shall eat your fill."

He took him to the palace bakery. The king had called in all the flour in the kingdom, and it had been baked into a huge bread mountain. But the man from the forest just went up to it and started eating, and by the end of the day it was all gone.

"Now can I marry her?" said Dimwit to the king.

"There's one last thing," the king replied. "You must come and fetch her on a ship that sails both on land and on water."

Dimwit went back to the forest, and this time he found the little old white-haired man, who said, "When I was hungry and thirsty, you shared your food and drink with me. Now that you need my help, I will give it, because you were kind to me." And the little old man gave him a ship that could sail in the air over both land and water.

When the king saw Dimwit sailing through the air towards the palace, he knew that he would have to keep his word. So Dimwit and the princess were married and lived happily together, because he could always make her laugh. And after the king died, Dimwit inherited his kingdom.

ALL TOGETHER NOW

"Where are you off to?"

"I'm off to market."

"You to market? Me to market. All together now, bow-wow-wow!"

"Got a man?"

"His name's Dan."

"Your man Dan? My man Dan. You to market? Me to market. All together now, bow-wow-wow!"

"Got a boy?"

"His name's Roy."

"Your boy Roy? My boy Roy. Your man Dan? My man Dan. You to market? Me to market. All together now, bow-wow-wow!"

"Got a girl?"

"I call her Shirl."

"Your girl Shirl? My girl Shirl. Your boy Roy? My boy Roy.

Your man Dan? My man Dan. You to market? Me to market. All together now, bow-wow-wow!"

"Got a name?"

"I'm-not-to-blame."

"Ain't it a shame! You're-not-to-blame? I'm-not-to-blame. Your girl Shirl? My girl Shirl. Your boy Roy? My boy Roy. Your man Dan? My man Dan. You to market? Me to market. All together now, bow-wow-wow!"

THE KNAPSACK,
THE HAT,
AND THE HORN

There were once three brothers who grew poorer and poorer until at last they were starving and didn't have a scrap of food in the house. "We can't go on like this," they said. "Let's go out into the world and seek our fortune."

They set off and they walked and walked. They tramped over many a blade of grass, but did not meet with any good fortune, till one day, walking through a forest, they came to a great mountain of silver. The eldest brother said, "That's good enough fortune for me. I don't ask for more." He took as much of the silver as he could carry, and went home. But the other two said, "We expect more from fortune than mere silver," and they carried on their way.

After another two days they came to a mountain of gold. The second brother couldn't make up his mind. "What should I do?" he asked himself. "Take enough gold to set myself up for life, or carry on?" At last he decided. He filled his pockets with gold, said

98

goodbye to his brother, and went home.

But the third said, "Silver and gold don't satisfy me. I'll carry on seeking my fortune, in the hope of something better still."

He went on, and when had walked for three days he came to a forest even larger than before. It seemed endless. As he could find nothing to eat or drink, he began to feel faint. He climbed a tall tree to look for the end of the forest, but there were just treetops as far as the eye could see. As he came down the tree he was overcome with hunger pains. He thought, *If only I could find some food. I could eat the world!*

When he got down to the ground he was amazed to see a cloth-covered table laden with food. Steam was rising from the dishes, and his nose twitched. "My wish has come true," he said, "and just in time!"

Without asking where the food had come from or who had cooked it, he set to and ate until he couldn't eat any more. When he was done, he thought, *It's a shame to leave such a pretty tablecloth to rot in the forest*, and he folded it up and put it in his pocket. Then he went on his way.

That evening, he unfolded the tablecloth and, as he was hungry once more, said, "I wish you were covered with good things to eat again." No sooner had the wish crossed his lips than the tablecloth was crammed with tempting dishes. "Now I know what kitchen my food is cooked in," he said; for he saw that it was a magic tablecloth. "I shall treasure you more than mountains of silver and gold," he said. But still he felt that fortune might hold more than just a tablecloth, so he decided to carry on.

One night in a lonely wood he met a grimy charcoal burner,

who was cooking some potatoes over a fire. "Good evening, blackbird," he said. "What's life like, out here on your own?"

"One day's much like another," said the charcoal burner, "and every evening potatoes! Will you join me?"

"Thanks," he replied, "but I don't want to take the food from your mouth. If you'll bear with me, you shall be my guest."

"Are we going to eat air?" said the charcoal burner. "I can see you're not carrying any food, and there's nowhere for miles around to get any."

"Don't worry," came the reply. "You'll eat like a king." And he took out the cloth and ordered it to cover itself with food. In a flash it was laden with roasts and stews, as piping hot as if they came straight from the kitchen. The charcoal burner just sat and gaped.

"Come on, blackbird. Don't just sit there with your mouth hanging open. Fill it with food!" And the charcoal burner didn't need telling twice.

When they had scoffed up everything on the cloth, the charcoal burner said, "That cloth's a piece of all right. It would be just the ticket for me out here in the woods, with no one to cook for me. Would you swap it? There's a shabby old soldier's knapsack hanging over there that I have no use for anymore. It has magic powers, and I will trade it for your tablecloth."

"What magic powers?"

"I'm coming to that. All you have to do is give the knapsack a slap with your hand, and up pops a corporal with six men armed to the teeth, and they'll do whatever you tell them."

"I'm willing if you are," said the youngest brother. He gave the charcoal burner the tablecloth, slung the knapsack over his shoulder, and set off.

It wasn't long before he stopped to try out the knapsack. He slapped it, and out stepped the seven tough soldiers. The corporal saluted, barking, "At your bidding, sir!"

"Go back to the charcoal burner and make him give my tablecloth back, and be quick about it."

The soldiers turned about-face and quick-marched back to the charcoal burner, who gave up the cloth without a fight.

The young man dismissed the soldiers and walked on his way, wondering what else fortune would bring.

At sunset he came to another charcoal burner, who was cooking his supper over an open fire. "If you'd like some potatoes with salt but no dripping, you're welcome to join me," the fellow said.

"No, you join me," replied the young man, and he spread the tablecloth. It was instantly covered in delicious food. They ate and drank with relish, and afterwards the charcoal burner said, "I've got an old worn-out hat with magic powers. If you put it on and turn it around, it starts firing like a dozen cannons. It flattens everything in sight; nothing can withstand it. It's no use to me, and I'd gladly swap it for your tablecloth."

"That's fine by me," said the young man. He took the hat and put it on, and left the tablecloth in exchange. But he hadn't walked far before he slapped the knapsack and ordered the soldiers to get the tablecloth back.

"Luck breeds luck!" he said to himself. "And there may be more to come." He could feel he was on a roll.

At the end of another day's walk, he came to a third charcoal burner, who like the first two offered to share his potatoes. Once more the young man brought out his cloth and invited the fellow to dine.

The charcoal burner enjoyed his meal so much that he offered to trade a magic horn for the cloth. This horn had very different properties from those of the hat. When you blew it, walls and fortifications just fell down, and towns and villages could be reduced to ruins. The young man took the horn, and gave the charcoal burner the cloth, but then sent his soldiers back to fetch it, so that at last he had won the knapsack, the hat, and the horn without giving up the magic tablecloth.

"That's it," he said to himself. "I've made my fortune. Now it's time for me to go home and see how my brothers are getting along."

When he got home, he found that his brothers had built themselves a splendid house with their silver and gold, and were living high on the hog. He went to see them, but as he was wearing a ragged coat, wearing a shabby hat, and carrying a worn old knapsack, they refused to acknowledge him as their brother. They jeered at him, saying, "You can't fool us, pretending to be our brother. Silver and gold weren't good enough for him, oh no! *He* will come back as a king, not as a beggar." And they threw him out into the street.

He was so angry. He kept slapping his knapsack until a hundred and fifty soldiers stood before him. He told them to surround his brothers' house, and then he ordered two of them to cut hazel switches and beat his stuck-up brothers until they

remembered who he was.

There was a great hue and cry. People wanted to help the two brothers, but there was nothing they could do against the soldiers.

When the king heard what was going on, he was furious. He told a captain to march a company of troops into town and send the troublemaker packing. But the youngest brother just slapped more soldiers out of his knapsack, so that the captain and his troops were forced to retire with bloody noses.

The king said, "We'll have to teach this upstart a lesson," and the next day he sent out a whole battalion; but they did even worse. The youngest brother sent more troops against them and, to get the thing over with as quickly as possible, turned his hat round twice on his head, so that the cannons roared and the king's men were put to flight.

Then the young man said, "I won't make peace until the king sends me his daughter to be my wife and lets me govern the kingdom in his name."

The king told his daughter, "It's a hard pill to swallow, but I must do as he says. If I want peace and want to keep my crown on my head, I must hand you over to him."

So the wedding was celebrated, but the king's daughter was very miffed to be married to a commoner with a shabby hat and a worn old knapsack. She racked her brains day and night to think how to get rid of him. She wondered, *Could his magic powers lie in his knapsack?* She wheedled around him, and when his heart had been softened by her kisses and caresses, said, "If only you would take off that ugly knapsack. It makes you look such a sight."

"Dear child," he said, "that knapsack is my greatest treasure. As long as I have it, I need fear no power on earth." And he told her its secret.

She threw her arms around him as if to kiss him, and quickly slipped the knapsack off his shoulders and ran away with it. As soon as she was alone she slapped it, and ordered the soldiers to arrest their former master and take him out of the palace. When they had gone, she slapped still more soldiers out of the knapsack and sent them too, with orders to drive him out of the country.

He would have been lost if he hadn't had the hat. The moment the soldiers let go his hands, he turned it twice. The cannons roared, and began to smash the palace to bits. The king's daughter herself had to come and beg for mercy.

She pleaded with him so pathetically and with such pretty promises that he let her persuade him to make peace. After that she was so loving that he lost his head to her completely and even told her the secret of the hat.

When he was asleep, she took his hat, and had him thrown out into the street.

But he still had his horn, and in his fury he blew it with all his might. Instantly the palace collapsed, and the king and his daughter were crushed to death.

If he had blown the horn just a little longer, everything would have been ruined, and not one stone would have been left standing on another.

No one dared stand up to him after that, so he made himself king over the whole country.

SNOW WHITE

Once in midwinter, when the snowflakes were falling like feathers from the sky, a queen sat sewing at a window, and the frame of the window was wrought of black ebony. And as she was sewing, and gazing at the falling snow, she pricked her finger with the needle, and three drops of blood fell on the snow. The red looked so striking on the snow that she said, "I wish I had a child as white as snow and as red as blood and as black as this window frame."

A short while after that, she gave birth to a daughter. Her skin was as white as snow, her lips and cheeks were as red as blood, and her hair was as black as ebony. They called her Snow White, and when she was born, the queen died.

A year later the king took a second wife. She was a beautiful woman, but proud and haughty, and she couldn't bear anyone else to be more beautiful than she was. She had a magic mirror, and when she looked in it she would say,

Mirror, mirror, on the wall,
Who is the fairest of them all?

and the mirror would answer,

You are the fairest of them all.

And then she would preen herself, because she knew the mirror spoke the truth.

But as Snow White grew, she became more and more beautiful. By the time she was seven years old she was as beautiful as the day and more beautiful than the queen. So one day when the queen said to her mirror,

Mirror, mirror, on the wall,
Who is the fairest of them all?

the mirror replied,

You are the fairest in this hall;
Snow White is the fairest of them all.

The queen turned yellow with shock and green with envy. From that moment, whenever she looked at Snow White, her heart turned over in her breast, she hated the girl so much.

Envy and pride began to strangle her heart, like weeds in a flowerbed. She knew no peace, night or day. So at last she sent for a huntsman and told him, "Get that child out of my sight. Take her into the forest and kill her and bring me back her heart and her liver as proof."

The huntsman obeyed. He took the child into the forest, but when he had drawn his knife and was about to pierce Snow

White's innocent heart, she began to weep, and said, "Ah, dear huntsman, let me live! I will run away into the wild forest and never come home again."

As she was so beautiful, the huntsman took pity on her and said, "Run away, then, you poor child." And though he thought to himself, *The wild beasts will get her soon enough*, still he felt as if a stone had been rolled from his heart, as he no longer had to kill her. Just then a young boar came running by, and he stabbed it and cut out its heart and liver to take to the queen as proof that the child was dead. And the wicked queen ordered the cook to stew them with salt, and she ate them, thinking she was eating the heart and liver of poor Snow White.

Meanwhile Snow White was all alone in the forest. She didn't know what to do. She was even afraid of the leaves on the trees. She started to run over sharp stones and through spiky thorns, and the wild beasts ran past her and did her no harm.

She ran as far as her legs would carry her. Then, just as night fell, she came to a little cottage and went inside to rest. Inside, everything was small, but so neat and clean. There was a table with a white cloth, and on it were laid seven little plates, each with its own knife, fork, spoon, and mug. Against the wall were seven little beds, all in a row, covered with white linen.

Snow White was very hungry and thirsty, but she did not want to eat all of anyone's meal. So she ate some from each plate, and drank some from each mug. Then, as she was so tired, she laid down on each of the beds in turn, until she found one that suited her, the seventh. Then she said a prayer and fell asleep.

When it was quite dark, the owners of the cottage came back.

They were seven dwarfs who mined the mountains for silver and gold. They lit their seven candles, and when they could see, each saw that something had been moved.

The first said, "Who's been sitting in my chair?"

The second said, "Who's been eating off my plate?"

The third said, "Who's been using my spoon?"

The fourth said, "Who's been using my fork?"

The fifth said, "Who's been using my knife?"

The sixth said, "Who's been drinking from my mug?"

And the seventh said, "Who's that sleeping in my bed?"

He called the others over, and they came running to see. The light from their candles fell on little Snow White as she lay there fast asleep, and they whispered, "What a lovely child!" and took care not to wake her. The seventh dwarf slept with the others, one hour with each in turn, and so the night passed.

In the morning, Snow White woke and was frightened when she saw the seven dwarfs. But they were friendly and asked her, "What's your name?"

"My name is Snow White," she said.

"And how do you come to be in our house?"

And she told them how her stepmother wanted to have her killed but the huntsman had spared her life, and how she had run all day through the forest until she came to their cottage.

The dwarfs said, "If you will take care of the house for us—do the cooking, make the beds, wash, sew, and knit, and keep everything neat and clean—you can stay with us, and we will look after you."

"Oh yes," said Snow White. "I'd love to."

So she stayed and looked after the house while the dwarfs went off to dig and delve, and in the evening when they came home she had a warm supper ready for them. She was alone all day, so the kindly dwarfs warned her, "Beware of your step-mother. She may find out you are here, so don't let anyone in."

Believing that she had eaten Snow White's heart and liver, the queen was sure that she was once more the most beautiful of all. But when she asked her mirror,

> *Mirror, mirror, on the wall,*
> *Who is the fairest of them all?*

it replied,

> *You are the fairest in this hall;*
> *Snow White is the fairest of them all.*
> *Beyond the forest and over the hills,*
> *With the seven dwarfs she dwells.*

The queen was taken aback, but she knew that the mirror never lied. She realized that the huntsman must have deceived her and that Snow White must still be alive.

She thought and thought how she might kill her—for until she was once again the fairest in the land, envy would eat her up. At last she made a plan. She dressed up as an old pedlar woman and made up her face so that you would never have known it was her. She crossed the mountains in disguise and came to the house of the seven dwarfs. She knocked at the door, crying, "Pretty things for sale! Going cheap!"

Snow White looked out of the window, and called, "Hello, old woman. What have you got to sell?"

"Nice things, nice things," she answered. "Stay-laces woven of bright silk." And she pulled out one of the pretty laces.

Snow White thought, *This old woman has an honest face. I can let her in*. And she opened the door to her and bought a lace.

"Child," said the old woman, "you look a fright. Let me lace you properly."

Snow White stood and let her put in the new lace. But the old woman laced her so quickly and tightly that she couldn't breathe, and she fell down as if dead.

"Now I am the most beautiful," said the queen, and she hurried away.

Shortly the seven dwarfs came home. What a shock they had, to find Snow White lying on the floor! She wasn't breathing, and they thought she was dead.

They lifted her up and, seeing how tightly she was laced, cut the lace. She took in a little breath and, little by little, she came to life again. When the dwarfs heard what had happened, they said, "The old pedlar woman must have been the queen in disguise. You've got to be careful and not let anyone in when we are not here."

When the wicked woman got home, she stood in front of her mirror and asked,

> *Mirror, mirror, on the wall,*
> *Who is the fairest of them all?*

It replied,

You are the fairest in this hall;
Snow White is the fairest of them all.
Beyond the forest and over the hills,
With the seven dwarfs she dwells.

When she heard that, all her blood rushed to her heart with hatred. So Snow White was still alive! "Never mind," she said, "I'll think of something." She thought over all her worst spells, and then, muttering under her breath, she made a poisoned comb.

Then she disguised herself as another old woman. She made her way across the hills to the house of the seven dwarfs and knocked at the door, crying, "Pretty things for sale! Going cheap!"

Snow White looked out of the window, and called, "Go away! I can't let anyone in."

"But there's no harm in looking, is there?" said the old woman, and she held up the poisoned comb.

It was so pretty that Snow White thought, *This old woman seems harmless. I can let her in.*

She opened the door, and the old woman said, "You hair is all tangled. Let me comb it for you." Snow White stood there patiently, and the old woman jabbed the poisoned comb into her hair. As soon as it touched her, Snow White fell down senseless. "Much good may your beauty do you now," said the wicked woman. "You are done for." And she went away.

It wasn't long before the dwarfs came home. When they saw Snow White lying as if dead, they at once suspected her stepmother. They checked her over, and found the poisoned comb. When they took it out, Snow White began to come to. She told them what had happened, and they warned her again to take care and not to open the door to anyone.

When the queen got home, she went straight to her mirror.

> *Mirror, mirror, on the wall,*
> *Who is the fairest of them all?*

It replied,

> *You are the fairest in this hall;*
> *Snow White is the fairest of them all.*
> *Beyond the forest and over the hills,*
> *With the seven dwarfs she dwells.*

When she heard the mirror speak, she trembled and shook with rage. "Snow White must die!" she shrieked. "Even if it costs me my life." Then she went to her secret room and made a poisonous apple. It was white with a red cheek, and looked so delicious that anyone would have been tempted; but whoever ate even the tiniest piece of it would die.

When the apple was ready, she made up her face and disguised herself as another old woman and made her way across the hills to the house of the seven dwarfs. She knocked at the door, and Snow White put her head out of the window straight away, and said, "I can't let anyone in. The seven dwarfs told me not to."

"It's all the same to me," said the old woman. "I'm just giving away apples. Here, have one."

"No," said Snow White. "I daren't."

"Are you afraid of poison?" said the old woman. "Look, I'll cut the apple in two. You have the red cheek, and I'll have the white." The apple was so cunningly made that only the red cheek was poisonous.

Snow White longed for the apple, it looked so perfect, and when she saw the old woman eating the white half she couldn't resist. She reached out and took the poisonous half. As soon as she bit into it, she fell down dead.

The queen gave her a cruel look, and cackled, "White as snow, red as blood, black as ebony! This time the dwarfs cannot wake you up!"

This time when she asked her mirror,

> *Mirror, mirror, on the wall,*
> *Who is the fairest of them all?*

the mirror replied,

> *You are the fairest of them all.*

Then her envious heart was at peace—as much as an envious heart can ever be.

When the dwarfs came home that evening they found Snow White lying lifeless on the ground. They lifted her up, searched her for anything poisonous, unlaced her, combed her, washed her with water and wine, but this time they could not revive her. The dear girl was dead, and dead she remained. They laid her on the table, and all seven of them sat around it and wept for three whole days.

Then they were going to bury her, but she still looked as if she were alive, with her beautiful red cheeks. They said, "We can't bury her in the dark ground." So they had a coffin made out of glass, so that she could be seen from all sides, and they laid her in it, and wrote her name on it in golden letters, and that she was a king's daughter. They they put the coffin on the top of the hill, and one of them always stayed by it to watch over it. And the birds came and wept for Snow White: first an owl, then a raven, then a dove.

Snow White lay there in her coffin for a long, long time. She didn't decay but lay as if she were asleep. She was still as white as snow, as red as blood, and as black as ebony.

One day, a prince came into the forest, and spent the night at the house of the seven dwarfs. He saw the coffin on the hilltop and the beautiful Snow White inside it, and he read what was written on it in golden letters. Then he said to the dwarfs, "Let me have the coffin. I will give you whatever you want for it."

"We wouldn't part with it for all the money in the world," they replied.

Then he said, "Then let me have it as a gift, for I can't live without being able to gaze on Snow White. I will love her forever."

Then the dwarfs took pity on him and gave him the coffin.

The prince's servants picked up the coffin to carry it away on their shoulders. One of them tripped over a tree stump, and the jolt shook the poisoned apple from Snow White's throat, where it had lodged. So before long she opened her eyes, lifted the glass lid of the coffin, and sat up. She was alive again!

"Oh!" she cried. "Where am I?"

The prince was filled with joy. "You are with me," he said, "and I love you more than the whole world. Come with me to my father's palace and be my wife."

As soon as she saw him, Snow White loved him too. She went with him, and soon they held their wedding feast.

Snow White's wicked stepmother was invited. When she had put on all her finery, she stood in front of her mirror and asked,

> *Mirror, mirror, on the wall,*
> *Who is the fairest of them all?*

And the mirror replied,

> *You are the fairest in this hall;*
> *The bride is the fairest of them all.*

The wicked woman spat out a curse. She was so wretched she didn't know what to do. At first she didn't want to go to the wedding, but she couldn't help it. She just had to go and see the prince's bride.

As soon as she saw her, she recognized Snow White. She wanted to run, but she couldn't move for rage and fear.

Iron slippers had been put into the fire. They were fetched out with tongs, and set before her. Her own envy and shame forced her feet into the red-hot shoes, and she danced in them until she dropped down dead.

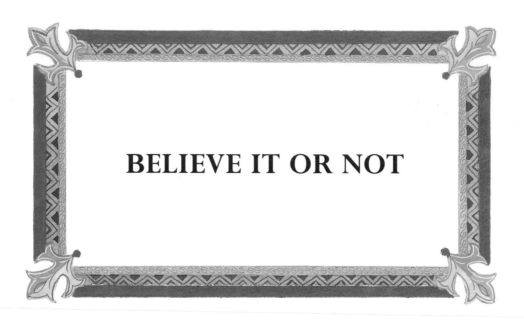

BELIEVE IT OR NOT

Listen, and you might learn something!

I saw two roast chickens flying along, their breasts to heaven and their backs to hell. I did.

I saw an anvil and a millstone swimming across the Rhine; they took their time about it, too. Ask the frog, if you don't believe me. He was sitting on the ice, quietly munching a cartwheel.

I saw a deaf man, a blind man, a dumb man, and a lame man catch a hare. The deaf man heard it coming, the blind man spotted it, the dumb man shouted, "There he goes!" and the lame man ran and caught it by the collar.

Over their heads, I saw three men in a sailing boat, its sails billowing in the wind. Up, up they went, but at last they rose too high, and were drowned.

I saw a crab catch a mouse, and a cow climb a house. In that country, the goats are as big as flies. . . .

Phew! Open the window, and let out the lies.

THE WATER OF LIFE

There was once a king who was so sick, everyone thought he was going to die. His three sons were very sad. They sat in the palace garden and wept. There they met an old man who asked them what the trouble was. They told him their father was very ill and would surely die. The old man said, "I know of a cure, and that is the water of life. If he drinks some of that, he will get well again. But it is hard to find."

The eldest son said, "I will find it." He went to the sick king and asked leave to go and search for the water of life. "No," said the king, even though it might cure him. "It's too dangerous." But the son begged and pleaded until the king gave his consent. For the prince thought in his heart, *If I bring him the water of life, my father will love me best, and I shall inherit the kingdom.*

So he set out, and on his journey he met a dwarf, who asked him, "Where are you going so fast?"

"What's it to you, you little runt?" said the proud prince.

119

So the dwarf cast a spell on him, so that he rode into a narrow ravine and got stuck. He could not move forwards or backwards, but was confined as tightly as if he were in prison.

The sick king waited and waited for him to return. When he did not, the second son begged leave to go and look for the water of life. He too thought, *If I find the water, then the kingdom will fall to me.*

The second son also met the dwarf, and dealt with him just as high-handedly. So the dwarf cast a spell on him, so that he too rode into a ravine and could not escape. That's the fate of haughty people.

When the second son did not return, the youngest begged to be allowed to go and seek the water of life. He thought, *I can save my father and my brothers too.*

When the dwarf asked him, "Where are you going so fast?" he told him, "My father is dying, and I am seeking the water of life, to cure him."

"Do you know where to look?" asked the dwarf.

"No," admitted the prince.

"As you have spoken kindly, and not haughtily like your brothers, I will help you. Soon you will reach a castle. In its courtyard is a fountain, and from that fountain springs the water of life. But it is an enchanted castle, and you will not be able to enter without this iron wand and two loaves of bread, which I will give you. You must strike the castle's iron door three times with the iron wand, and it will open. Inside are two lions with gaping jaws. You must throw each of them a loaf, and they will be quieted. Then hurry and collect some of the water of life before the clock strikes twelve, or you will be shut in again and never get out."

The prince thanked him for this advice, took the wand and the bread, and went on his way. When he reached the castle, everything was as the dwarf said. The door sprang open at the third stroke of the wand, and when he had quieted the lions with the bread, he made his way into the castle.

He came to a large, splendid hall full of enchanted princes. He took the rings from their fingers, and also a sword and a loaf of bread that he found there. Beyond the hall was a room in which he found a beautiful girl. She was overjoyed to see him. She kissed him and told him that he had set her free. "My kingdom will be yours," she said. "Return in a year, and we shall be married. But hurry now, and collect the water of life before it strikes twelve."

He went on through the castle, and came to a bedchamber with a beautiful newly made bed in it. He was very tired, so he lay down for a little rest. He fell fast asleep, and when he awoke, the clock was striking a quarter to twelve. He jumped up in a fright, ran to the spring, drew some water in a cup that he found there, and hurried away. As he was escaping through the iron door of the castle, the clock struck twelve, and the door came crashing down so fast it cut off a piece of his heel.

He was delighted to have found the water of life, and set off for home. On the way he met the dwarf. When the dwarf saw the sword and the loaf he said, "Those are great treasures. With the sword you can slay whole armies, and the loaf will never be finished, no matter how much you eat."

But the prince was only interested in finding his brothers. "What has happened to them?" he asked. "They set out in search of the water of life before I did, but they have not returned."

"They're stuck in ravines," said the dwarf. "I sent them there because they were so proud and overbearing."

The prince begged the dwarf to release them, and he agreed. But he warned, "Do not trust them. They have wicked hearts."

When his brothers joined him, he was glad to see them all the same. He told them all about his adventures, and how he had found the water of life, and brought a cupful away with him, and how he had freed a beautiful princess from enchantment, and how she was waiting for him and in a year they were to be wed, and he was to have her kingdom for his own.

On their way they passed through three kingdoms in which war and famine were raging. In each of them, the young prince lent the king of the country his sword, in order to defeat his enemies, and the loaf, in order to feed the people. Then they got on a boat and sailed for home.

The two older princes got together on the voyage and said, "Our brother has found the water of life, not us. For that our father will give him the kingdom. It should be ours by rights. He is nothing but a thief." And so they plotted to destroy him. They waited until he was asleep, and then they stole the water of life from the cup and replaced it with salt seawater.

As soon as they arrived home, the young prince took the cup to the king, expecting him to drink it and be cured. But as it was seawater, it made him worse than ever. As he was retching, the two older princes came to him and told them they feared their brother had tried to poison him. Then they gave him the true water of life.

As soon as the king drank the water, he was cured.

After that, the king made much of his two older sons but distrusted the younger. The older princes even bragged to their brother how they had deceived him, but there was nothing he could do about it, for his father would not have believed a word of it.

Thinking that the young prince had tried to murder him, the king decided he must die. He ordered his huntsman to shoot the prince when they were riding in the forest. But the man could not bring himself to do it and warned the prince to stay away from court.

The king was happy to think that his son was dead. But then three wagons of gold and jewels arrived, all for his youngest son. They were presents from the grateful kings of the three kingdoms that he had saved from war and famine. Then the king wondered, *What if I was wrong? What if he was innocent after all?* And he spoke aloud, "I wish he were still alive and that I had not ordered him killed!"

The huntsman heard these words and confessed to the king that he had not carried out the order but had let the prince go. At that a weight fell from the king's heart. He had it proclaimed in every country that his son was free to come home again.

Meanwhile the princess had ordered a golden road to be built leading to her castle, and told her guards, "The man who rides right up the middle of this road is the man for me. Anyone who rides alongside it is a liar, and you are not to let him in."

When the year was nearly over, the eldest son thought he would seek out the princess and pretend to be her rescuer. When he came to the gleaming golden road, he thought, *It would be a shame to mark this road by riding over it*, so he rode his horse along the verge. When he came to the iron door of the castle, the servants would not let him in.

Then the second prince set out, but he too thought it would be a shame to ride over the magnificent golden road, and rode along the verge. So the servants would not let him in either.

When the year was quite over, the youngest son remembered the princess who was waiting for him and set off to find her. When he came to the golden road, he saw it shining right up to the castle gate, and said to himself, *This will lead me to my love*. He rode his horse right up the middle of the road to the castle gates, and the servants let him in.

The princess welcomed him with joy, and they were married straightaway. She told him that he was now lord of all her kingdom. "But first, you must go to your father, who has forgiven you, and tell him all that has happened." So he rode home, and told the king how his brothers had betrayed him. The old king wanted to punish them, but they had fled to sea in a ship, and they never came back as long as they lived.

THE FISHERMAN
AND HIS WIFE

There was once a fisherman who lived with his wife in a pigsty by the sea. He went fishing every day; and he fished, and he fished.

One day he was sitting with his rod and line, looking into the clear water. And he sat, and he sat.

His line suddenly sank, down, down to the bottom of the sea, and when he pulled it up he had caught a large flounder. And the flounder said, "Listen. I'm not really a flounder. I'm an enchanted prince. So there's no point in killing me—I wouldn't be good to eat. Put me back in the water and let me go."

"There's no need to go on," said the fisherman. "If you can talk, you can go free." And he released the flounder back into the sea, and it swam down to the bottom, leaving a streak of blood behind it. Then the fisherman called it a day, and went home to his wife in the pigsty.

"Have you caught nothing at all today?" she asked.

"No," he said. "I did catch a flounder, but it turned out to be an enchanted prince, so I let it go."

"Didn't you make a wish first?"

"No," he said. "What would I wish for?"

"What about somewhere better to live than this filthy pigsty? You could have wished for a little cottage. Go and catch him again, and wish for a cottage. He couldn't deny us that."

"I'm not sure about that," said the fisherman.

"Well I am," said his wife. "Off you go right this minute and catch that flounder." He didn't really want to go, but he knew better than to disobey his wife, so he went.

When he got there the sea was all green and yellow, and no longer crystal clear. He stood on the shore, and said,

> *Flounder, flounder in the sea,*
> *Come, come, come to me;*
> *For my wife, good Ilsabil,*
> *Has sent me here, against my will.*

Then the flounder came swimming to him and said, "What does she want?"

"She says that as I caught you, I should have wished for something. She doesn't want to live in a pigsty anymore. She wants a cottage."

"Go home then," said the flounder. "She has it already."

When the man got home his wife was no longer in the pigsty, but in a little cottage. She was sitting on a bench just inside the door. She took him by the hand, and led him through the porch and into the sitting room and the bedroom and the kitchen and the pantry, all the while exclaiming, "Isn't this better?" Best of all was the yard with hens and ducks, and a little garden full of fruit and vegetables. "Isn't it lovely?" said the wife.

"Yes," said fisherman. "It'll do us nicely. We shall be snug as a bug in a rug."

"We'll see," said the wife, and they went off to bed.

All went well for a couple of weeks, but then the wife began to feel dissatisfied. "This cottage is too poky," she said, "and the yard's just a pocket handkerchief. It would have been just as easy for the flounder to give us a bigger house. I fancy a stone castle. Go and tell the flounder to give us a castle."

"I like the cottage," said the fisherman. "What would we want with a castle?"

"Just go and tell him."

"He's only just given us a cottage. I don't like to harass him."

"Go," said the wife. "He'll be glad to do it."

The man's heart was heavy. He said to himself, *It's not right*, yet he went. When he came to the sea, the water was purple and dark blue, quite murky and thick, but not stirred up. He stood on the shore and said,

> *Flounder, flounder in the sea,*
> *Come, come, come to me.*
> *For my wife, good Ilsabil,*
> *Has sent me here against my will.*

"What does she want now?" asked the flounder.

"She wants to live in a big stone castle," said the fisherman, all in a fluster.

"Just go home," said the flounder. "She's standing at the door."

So he set off for home, but it wasn't there anymore. He came to a great stone castle, with a huge stone staircase leading to the door, and at the top of the staircase was his wife. She took him by the hand and led him through the marble hall. Servants flung the doors open, and every room was bright with tapestries. The tables and chairs were made of pure gold. There were crystal chandeliers hanging from the ceilings, and fine rugs on the bedroom floors. It was almost too much to take in.

Behind the castle there was a great courtyard, with stables and carriages, and a flower garden, and rolling parkland with a herd of deer in it. It was everything the heart could desire.

"Isn't it wonderful?" said the wife.

"Yes," said the fisherman. "It's beautiful. We shall be happy here."

"We'll see," said the wife, and they went to bed.

Next morning the wife woke first. Day was breaking, and from her bed she could see the beautiful countryside around her. Her husband was still stretching when she poked him in the ribs and said, "Husband, look out of the window. Do you see all that country? We could be king over that. Go to the flounder and tell him we want to be king."

"Why should we want to be king?" said the husband. "I don't want to be king."

"Well," said the wife, "if you don't want to be king, I do. So go to the flounder. I will be king!"

"I can't tell him that," said the man. "Why do you want to be king? Why?"

"Because," said the wife. "Now get going. I must be king."

The husband went, and although he wasn't at all happy about it. *It's not right. It's not right*, he thought.

When he came to the sea, it was as dark as charcoal. The water was choppy, and it smelled vile. He went to the shore, and said,

> *Flounder, flounder in the sea,*
> *Come, come, come to me.*
> *For my wife, good Ilsabil,*
> *Has sent me here against my will.*

"What does she want now?" said the flounder.

"She wants to be king."

"The crown is already on her head."

The man went home, and when he got there the castle had become a huge palace with a tower and carvings. There were soldiers with drums and trumpets, and a sentry at the gate. When he went inside, everything was made of marble and gold, with velvet covers and great golden tassels.

The doors of the great hall were open wide, and his wife was holding court from a high throne of gold and diamonds, with a big gold crown on her head. Ladies-in-waiting stood in rows on both sides of her, each a head shorter than the last.

He went and stood before her, and said, "So, wife, you are king."

"Yes," she said. "Now I am king."

Then he stood and looked at her for a while, and after he had finished looking, he said, "Let's leave it there, shall we?"

"No, no," said the wife, quite upset. "Already the time is hanging heavy on my hands. I can't stand still. Go to the flounder and tell him I want to be emperor."

"I can't say that," said the husband. "How could he make you emperor? There's only one emperor in the empire. He can't do it, I tell you."

"What!" said the wife. "I am the king, and you are nothing but my husband. Don't argue with me—just go at once. If the flounder can make me king, he can make me emperor. Go!"

The man went, but he was very troubled. *Emperor!* he thought. *Emperor is too much. It won't end well. The flounder must be getting sick of this.*

When he came to the sea, it was black and turbid. It was churning up from below, and a sharp wind was whipping it into foam. The man was afraid. But he stood on the shore and said,

> *Flounder, flounder in the sea,*
> *Come, come, come to me.*
> *For my wife, good Ilsabil,*
> *Has sent me here against my will.*

"What's she after now?" said the flounder.

"I'm sorry, but she wants to be emperor."

"Go to her," said the flounder, "she is emperor already."

So he went home, and this time the whole palace was made of polished marble, with golden statues. The soldiers were marching up and down outside, blowing trumpets and beating drums,

133

and inside, barons, counts, and dukes were acting as servants. They opened the doors for him, and the doors were of pure gold. He found his wife on a throne made out of one block of gold, and it was at least two miles high. She was wearing a great golden crown set with precious stones, and clutching the imperial orb. On either side of her stood a row of guards, each one shorter than the one next to him, from the biggest giant, who was two miles high, to the smallest dwarf, who was no bigger than a finger. Dukes and princes were crowding around her.

The fisherman went and stood alongside them, and said, "So you're emperor now."

"Yes," she said, "I'm emperor."

"Well, you can't go higher than that."

"Oh yes I can," she said. "Now that I'm emperor, I want to be pope too."

"I can't ask the flounder that!" said the husband in alarm. "No, no, you can't be pope. There's only one pope."

"Fiddle-faddle!" she said. "I'm the emperor, and you're only my husband. Go at once to the flounder and tell him I want to be pope."

He felt quite weak in the knees, but he went. He shivered. A cold wind was blowing, and the clouds were flying. It grew dark, and the gusts of wind tore the leaves from the trees. The water roared and foamed as if it were boiling, and the waves crashed against the shore. Out at sea, boats were firing distress flares. There was still a patch of blue in the sky, but mostly it was the fierce red of an angry storm. He stood on the shore in fear and despair, and said,

Flounder, flounder, in the sea,
Come, come, come to me.
For my wife, good Ilsabil,
Has sent me her against my will.

"Well, what does she want?" said the flounder.

"I'm afraid she wants to be pope."

"Go home," said the flounder. "She is pope already."

When he got home, it was a huge cathedral surrounded by palaces. He pushed his way through the crowd. Inside, everything was lit by candles. His wife was dressed in gold, and was sitting on an even higher throne, with three golden crowns. Emperors and kings were on their knees before her, kissing her shoe.

"So," said the fisherman, "now you are pope."

"Yes," she said, "I am pope."

He stood and looked at her, and it was as if he were staring at the sun. When he had finished looking, he said, "I hope you'll be satisfied now. You can't do better than pope."

"We'll see," she said, and they went to bed.

But she couldn't sleep. She was restless and fretful. She couldn't stop thinking what else there was that she could be. All night she tossed and turned, but she couldn't come up with anything.

At sunrise, she saw the red glow of dawn through the window. And when she saw the sun rising, she thought, *Why can't I make the sun and moon rise?*

"Husband!" she shouted, poking him in the ribs with her

elbows, "Wake up! Go and see the flounder. I want to be God."

The fisherman was still half asleep, but her words gave him such a jolt that he fell out of bed. He thought he must have misheard. He rubbed his eyes, and said, "What's that?"

"If I can't make the sun and moon rise, I won't be able to bear it. I'll never have another moment's happiness if I can't make them rise." She shot him a look so mad it sent a shiver right through him. "Go at once. I want to be God."

The man flung himself to his knees. "Wife, the flounder can't do that. He can make an emperor and a pope. Please, I beg you, be content with pope."

She fell into a rage. Her hair stood on end, and she began to kick and scream. "I can't stand it," she cried. "I can't stand it for a moment longer. Go!"

He pulled on his trousers and ran wildly out. A storm was raging. The wind was blowing so hard that he could scarcely keep his feet. Trees and houses were falling, and even the mountains were trembling, sending great rocks crashing down into the sea. The sky was pitch black, but in the lightning flashes he could see black waves as big as mountains and as high as church towers, each with a crest of white foam. He couldn't hear his own voice, but he bellowed,

> *Flounder, flounder in the sea,*
> *Come, come, come to me.*
> *For my wife, good Ilsabil,*
> *Has sent me here against my will.*

"What can she want now?" said the flounder.

"She wants to be God," stammered the fisherman.

"Go home," said the flounder. "She's back in the pigsty."

And they are still living there to this day.

THE GOLDEN KEY

One shivering winter's day, when the snow lay thick on the ground, a poor boy was sent out into the forest to fetch wood. He gathered a good pile, but even hard work couldn't keep him warm on such a bitter day. His skin turned blue, his teeth were chattering—the poor lad was starved with cold. There was nothing for it but to start a fire.

So he scraped away the snow and cleared a space, and what did he find? A golden key.

"Where there's a key, there's a lock!" he said, and started to dig down into the frozen ground, and what did he find? A box.

"If only the key fits," he said, "my fortune is made!"

He looked for the lock, but he couldn't find it. He looked again, and there it was, a keyhole so tiny you could scarcely see it. He put the key in the lock, and it fitted perfectly.

He began to turn the key, and what did he find? We shall have to wait and see.

When he has turned it all the way and opened the lid, then we shall know what is in that box of delights.